David Line

SCREAMING HIGH

Little, Brown and Company
Boston   Toronto

FIRST AMERICAN EDITION

PRINTED IN GREAT BRITAIN

One

I was beating it fast through the park when I heard the screaming. It was the most terrible screaming. I thought jeeze, I'm not stopping here. There'd been a murder there not long before. A kid had been murdered. I thought if I see a keeper I'll tell him. They'd be shutting the gates soon, anyway.

Except just then it grew worse. It grew into a kind of shriek, with bitter crying. I thought boy, I can't go now. How can I just go and let it happen? I remembered hearing somewhere that if you disturbed a murderer he'd stop and run. I thought yeah, and he could run right at me.

I was scared out of my mind.

I stopped and looked round, though.

I couldn't see a soul. There was just a clump of trees near the lake. I knew the crying had to be coming from there so I tiptoed in, and all my skin turned to gooseflesh and all my hairs started bristling. I thought if I see anyone I'll yell; and if he comes at me I'll hide. I'll hide behind a tree. Except just then I recognized the crying. It turned to laughing anyway; but I kept on.

He couldn't see me. He was sitting facing the other way. He was sitting on the ground playing a trumpet.

The branches of the tree came down on all sides like a tent. It was so dark I could hardly see *him*.

He knew I was there, and stopped immediately.

"I wondered what it was," I said.

He didn't say anything.

"I wondered if it was trouble," I said.

He sat dead still.

"They're shutting the park."

He was looking towards, but not at, me. He had his head on one side as if listening to something beyond.

I said, "You want to stay here?"

He said, "You want to scram?"

The way he held his head he seemed blind, but I knew he wasn't. I could see him now. He was a kid at school called Ratbag. They called him that because he was a mess. He was a mess in every way. He never looked at you. He never said anything. He'd put a kid in hospital once, though, for mocking him so I said nothing more either. I just stepped back, and at the same moment heard the keepers bawling "Closing time!" and saw two of them bobbing through the trees. Ratbag saw them too, and he breathed a bit heavily and stood up.

I didn't see what he did with the trumpet. He had a backpack over his shoulders as we came out of the trees.

One of the keepers was coming over.

"You deaf?" he was yelling.

"Yeah, coming," I said.

"Well, get a move on."

He'd started staring at Ratbag.

Well, people did that.

It wasn't that he was black. He was just weird. He was

a freak. He had this little woolly hat. He had very long arms and legs that moved in a funny way like a wooden doll's.

"Look lively, then," the keeper growled.

He was walking behind us now, jangling his keys and muttering because we were going slowly. Ratbag was doing it deliberately, and he went even slower then. I couldn't speed up when he didn't so I kept pace with him till the gates slammed behind us, and then took off.

But I'd hardly moved before his skinny hand snaked out and grabbed me. It grabbed my shoulder, hard.

"What name?" he said. "Yours."

"Nick Sanders."

"My school, right?"

"Right."

"You saw no trumpet, bub."

"OK."

"I hear I have a trumpet, I know which person said that. I take that person apart," he said.

He still wasn't looking at me. He was staring blindly over my shoulder. I tried to shake him off but he just hung on tighter, grinding the shoulder.

"Understand?" he said.

"Yeah. All right. I said so!"

"Believe it," he said, and took off; and I walked home, burning.

I felt sick. I felt a fool, too. I thought how I'd gone to help him, and was sorry I'd done it. I thought he'd probably pinched the trumpet, and I hoped they'd get him for it. Then I hoped they wouldn't, or he'd get me.

I felt worse than ever. I started thinking what I ought

7

to have said or ought to have done. Also what I'd better do now. I thought if he tried to pick on me I'd see there were always people around, to scare him off. Except he didn't seem too scareable. Then I thought if anything did happen with the trumpet I'd have to convince him it wasn't me, explain how it couldn't be. Except he wasn't a person you could explain to, either.

I thought jeeze, what a jerk, what a pig.

I felt sick as hell about him. I really hated him.

I had tea when I got home and tried to think of homework. I thought of the trumpet instead. I'd never heard one that could laugh or cry before. I didn't know they could do it. I wondered how *he* could. I couldn't remember hearing a trumpet by itself before. I couldn't get over the strange sound of it in the dark.

I thought if he could do that with it he must have been able to play it pretty well to begin with, or there'd be no point in pinching it. Then I wondered why no one else knew he could play. They always wanted people for the band. If he had nothing else going for him he ought to have made the most of that.

I tried remembering what else I knew about him, but all I could think of was the kid he'd put in hospital. It wasn't a smaller kid but a big one, and nobody'd minded because the swine had it coming anyway. And Ratbag hadn't started it so he didn't get into trouble. In fact for a week or two he'd been quite popular, though he'd done nothing about it. He just kept out of everyone's way.

All you could say of him was that he was a mess. Even apart from his clothes – and I remembered he always wore two odd sneakers on his feet – he was a mess. He had a strange smell about him, like straw, as if he slept in it. He never seemed to know where he was. If a class had to turn up in one room, he'd turn up in another. He seemed half crazy.

He could play the trumpet, though. I couldn't get over it.

I wondered why he played it in the park. Then I thought, well if he pinched it where else could he play it?

I kept hearing the sound of it, screaming round my skull. Not just laughing and crying but screaming all kinds of things. Then I realized I was tackling the wrong problem, and the real one was not how he played but that if anyone else found out he'd be taking me apart.

That's the one I concentrated on.

I don't know if I started noticing him particularly, but wherever I was he seemed to be there suddenly. I'd see this little woolly hat. He'd be standing somewhere not quite looking at me. It began turning my stomach.

I came out the lunch room one day and read the notices on the board and turned round and there he was. Something seemed to jump in my throat and I said, "Look, did you want something?"

"Yeah," he said. He seemed surprised. His lips were pursed as if he was whistling, and he was looking over my shoulder. "Outside," he said.

"OK."

There were plenty of people outside, but my heart started thumping. He'd beat the other kid up outside.

We began walking round the yard, and he said, "You

followed me the other night, right?" He was nodding as if he'd already checked.

"No way."

"Right to my tree?" he said, still nodding.

"I told you why – I heard someone crying there."

"So?"

"I was going to help."

He gave me a look. It was the first time I'd seen his eyes properly. They were big ones, hysterical, like a horse's.

"The trumpet is mine," he said.

"OK."

"Don't get ideas about it."

"I never even thought of it."

"Only no one has to know it."

"Well, they won't from me," I told him.

He was looking at his two odd sneakers, one red, the other blue. He was stepping very high in them, like on a stony beach.

"You were going to *help*?" he said.

"Yeah, sort of."

"What way?"

I remembered I was going to jump behind a tree.

"Different ways," I said.

"It was like crying, eh?"

"Crying and laughing."

"Yeah, *right*!" He wriggled his bony shoulders and gave me another look, still hysterical, but different. "Right *on*!" he said, and suddenly giggled.

I was so surprised I said, "You been playing the trumpet long?"

"A while."

"You play in the park?"

"Different places."

"In the band?"

"*Nah!*"

He started dragging his feet and scowling.

"Well, who needs the band?" I said, and I said it fast in case he turned nasty again.

"No, it's, uh, the trumpet." He covered his mouth and gave a small embarrassed cough. "See, I couldn't show the *trumpet*."

"You couldn't play one of their trumpets?"

"Whose trumpets?"

"Hasn't the band got trumpets?"

"Trumpets they let you *play*?"

"Why wouldn't they?" I said.

He stopped and pursed his lips to whistle again.

"I never thought of it," he said.

He didn't look at me. He looked all round the yard. "Well, hot *dog*," he added.

The end of break signal sounded so we had to go then.

He said, "Hey, I'm sorry what I said."

"Forget it."

"It was, like, nice what you did, going to help."

"Yeah, I'm a hero," I said.

He looked at me a moment and suddenly giggled again.

"Hey, listen," he said.

"Ratbag, we got to go." Everyone had practically gone, but I suddenly realized what I'd called him and said, "Look, I didn't mean to call you – "

"What's a name?" he said. "I mean listen, suppose I did want to do something about that?"

"About what?"

"Like trying to ... *Nah.* I mean they'd never ... Anyway. Yeah," he said, and took off.

I watched him a moment. He was wriggling his shoulders and lifting his feet very high in the sneakers as if all the rocks on the beach had become suddenly immense. He seemed to be talking to himself as well.

Oh boy, I thought, that's a weirdo. That's a freak.

Two

I knew what he meant, though, and the same evening I saw Sammy Segal. He's a kid with a flute. He plays it in the band. He knows everything.

I said, "Sammy, have they got spare trumpets in the band for people who don't have their own?"

He likes to get things clear, Sammy.

He said, "You mean, if a person wants to play a trumpet, and he hasn't got a trumpet, can he play one of the band's trumpets?"

"Yeah, something like that," I said.

He makes you tired before you start.

"Can he play?"

"A bit."

"Does he take music?"

"I don't know."

"Does he read it?"

"He didn't say."

"Who is he?"

"Yeah, well goodbye," I said, "and for ever."

"Here, hang on!" Sammy said, and stared hard at me through his glasses. "I'll find out for you, then."

He came up next day. It was a Friday.

"I found out," he said.

He'd been to see the music teacher, Skinhead. (His real name's Skindle. He has a head of hair down to here.)

"Skinhead says we've got trumpets, and he wants more wind players. So if your bloke wants to turn up before band call on Monday, Skinhead will see him. Tell him to turn up at five."

"Here," I said, alarmed. "I didn't say make a date."

"Skinhead made it. What's the problem?"

I thought about it. The big one was to stop Ratbag taking me apart if he thought I'd been going round talking about trumpets, in particular about *him* and trumpets. I remembered his secretiveness, his reluctance to be with people.

"Who else would be there Monday?" I said cautiously.

"Nobody. The band doesn't turn up till half past. Skinhead just sorts out the music and has half an hour to himself." He was looking at me curiously. "Is something the matter with this kid?" he said.

"I'll find out."

I had to find him first.

And that was the craziest thing. Before, I couldn't get rid of him. Now he seemed to have vanished. I asked the kids in his class where he was, but they didn't know. So I asked where he lived, and they didn't know that either. They said he often didn't show on Friday.

I thought OK, I'll see him Monday.

Except I saw him before.

I saw him the same night.

We ran out of eggs so I had to skid round to the supermarket. I made it just before they shut. The shelves were being stacked for the following day, the big carts going there and back to the storeroom. I had to pass the storeroom and I looked in the swing doors and saw a woolly hat. So I looked again, and it was him. He was stacking crates in there. I poked my head in, surprised, and said, "Ratbag?"

He looked round and saw me, and looked away.

I called louder, "*Ratbag!*"

He came over fast, with a scared look.

"You don't come in here," he said.

"I was looking for you all day."

He took his hat off and wiped his face with it.

"Outside and round the back," he said.

I got the eggs and went outside and round the back.

He was already waiting there.

"What you want?" he said.

"You worked here all *day*?"

"What's it to you?"

"OK." I could see he was nervous. "About trumpets," I said, "you can play on Monday if you want. Skinhead will see you in the band room at five."

"What? *What*?" he said.

"Look, your name wasn't mentioned," I said. His eyes had begun rolling like a horse again. "It never even came up. I just got a friend to ask if they *had* trumpets, and he found out they needed wind players as well. So if you want ... "

I started telling him what Sammy had told me, but I don't know if he even heard.

"*Crazy, man. He's crazy!*" he muttered to himself. "*What does he understand?*" Then he took his hat off and

15

wiped his face again, and seemed to fly into a temper. "Look, stay away from me! Just leave me alone, eh?" He put his hat on again. "And get lost!" he said, and took off.

I looked after him a while, and took off myself.

I thought what a jerk, a pig, a freak. That was the second time I'd tried to help him, and the second time he turned me off.

Yeah well, and the last, I thought.

I didn't see him Monday, and I heard nothing either. On Tuesday Sammy said, "What happened to the trumpet man?"

"Didn't he show?"

"Skinhead said not."

"I don't know what happened," I said.

"So what was the mystery?"

"Whatever it was, it's over now."

Except it wasn't, of course. It just started again.

Wherever I was, he was there again suddenly, never quite looking at me. This time I didn't bother looking at him.

He must have followed me home one day. On Monday I came out the front door, and there he was on the doorstep.

He said, "Hey!" and screwed his hat on a bit tighter.

I never even looked at him. I just set off down the road, and he fell into step beside me.

"I'm sorry about what I said," he said softly.

I seemed to have heard this before.

"It was nice what you did."

I kept right on.

"You got a right to be annoyed."

"Look, Ratbag," I told him. "I'm not annoyed. I'm just sick of you. I don't want to know you."

"I got difficulties," he said.

"Well, hang on to them."

"I don't play the trumpet properly."

I looked at him.

"It sounded OK to me."

"Well, it ain't," he said.

He was scowling.

"See, it's like, to a person that knows – it's comical. The technique."

"I don't want to know," I told him.

"I produce a note, sure," he said, shaking his head. "Only a person that knows, he'd say that's an ignorant note, man. Who taught you to make that note?"

"Well, who did?" I said.

"That *kind* of question," he agreed.

He was wriggling his shoulders and stepping very high. He still had the odd sneakers on. I'd been wondering about them. I wondered why he didn't get himself a new pair. If he was in the habit of taking days off to work in the supermarket, he ought to have dough for a pair of sneakers. I didn't bother asking. He never answered questions anyway.

"See, suppose Skinhead says OK, take a trumpet and blow a note, man – what happens? I blow a note, yeah. And a great note. But I blow it the wrong way."

"Blow it some other way."

"I blow my way. But it always comes out great."

"Couldn't you make it look accidental?" It seemed a crazy question, but he took it seriously.

"It ain't accidental," he said quietly.

"Ratbag," I said, "don't think I care, because I don't. Only what's the problem? If you play some wrong way, and you want to play a right one, isn't Skinhead the guy to show you?"

"I couldn't handle the *questions*," he said. "Like, who showed you that, and which trumpet? I couldn't handle it. But I was wondering ... If someone else was there, someone who could fuzz up the answers if the questions got – "

"You mean you want me to come with you?" I said.

He started looking all round, pursing his lips.

"You don't have to," he said.

"Ratbag, I don't know if you noticed," I told him, "but every time I've done something nice for you, you've done something pretty stinking awful to me."

"Hey!" he said.

He seemed shocked. He started wriggling his shoulders, mumbling. "What you want to say that for?"

"I don't want you doing it again."

His whole body started wriggling, and he looked over my right ear and then my left, without once looking directly at me.

"You know I won't," he muttered.

"OK," I said. "I'll be nice to you one time more, Ratbag."

We went to the band room at five, and found Skinhead with his head down in the music.

Ratbag was so nervous he made me nervous.

"Sir," I said.

"M'm?" Skinhead said.

"The boy who wanted to play a trumpet, sir?"

"Which boy?"

"Last week, sir."

"What about him?"

"He's here now."

"What name?"

"Mountjoy," Ratbag said uneasily.

It was the first time I'd heard it and I looked at him. Skinhead looked at him too.

"OK," he said wearily and got up. He shook his great mane of hair and reached for a trumpet.

"Ever handle one of these, Mountjoy?"

"A bit, sir."

"Think you can get a note out of it?"

"Try, sir."

"Off you go."

Ratbag looked at the trumpet. Then he pursed his lips and raised it to his mouth.

"No, no," Skinhead said.

"Eh?" Ratbag said.

He hadn't done anything yet.

"Smile," Skinhead said.

"Smile?"

Skinhead picked up a trumpet and smiled himself. He stretched his lips in a weird kind of grin and put the trumpet up to it. After a couple of false starts something like a raspberry came out.

"Well, not so hot," he said, "but that's the idea. You

don't blow. You smile. What you've got here is a long piece of plumbing, all coiled up. You get a column of air going gently through it. These knobs that go up and down – leave them alone now – either block off or open up different sections of the plumbing to produce *notes*. That is, they vary the length of the column of *air*. All you have to do is keep the air going. But *gently*, eh? Got it, Mountjoy?"

"I think so," Ratbag said nervously.

"Off again, then."

Ratbag picked up the trumpet and pursed his lips.

"No blow!" Skinhead said warningly.

"Sir," I said. I was hanging on Ratbag's pullover. I thought he was going to take off. "Can he do it his way, sir? Just for starters."

"OK," Skinhead said.

Ratbag put the trumpet up again. He was so confused and frightened he didn't know whether to smile or blow. I don't know what he did but a confused and frightened sound came out. It came out right away, without any false starts. It was like an animal yelping in alarm; but at the same time funny as if the animal, even while yelping, knew it was only a mock yelp, a kind of comical one. There were dozens of notes in the yelp, and his fingers flashed over the knobs, but it only took him two or three seconds. I don't know how he managed it.

Skinhead stared at him.

"Now that," he said, "is something that every now and again does happen with a beginner on the trumpet. You did absolutely everything wrong but still managed to get some quite decent notes. Pure luck! You could try for years and never manage it again. Go on, see if I'm right."

Ratbag raised the trumpet and blew the same yelp.

He blew exactly the same one.

Skinhead's mouth dropped open.

"Mountjoy," he said, "have you done that before?"

"Well, only when you told me," Ratbag said.

"That high note – the one near the beginning. Can you manage that one just on its own?"

Ratbag blew the high note on its own.

"Now the one near the end, not quite so high."

Ratbag blew that one, too.

Skinhead had turned quite pale.

"Mountjoy," he said, "I want to try something with you." He walked over to the piano and tapped a note. "Could you do that on the trumpet?"

"Well I could," Ratbag said, frowning. "But it's flat."

"Flat?" Skinhead said. "The piano's just been tuned."

He tapped a few times more, humming. Then he got a tuning fork and sounded it. Then he tapped the note again.

"Well, I'm damned," he said. "It *is* flat. Slightly. *Very* slightly." He left the piano and came and looked at Ratbag. "Mountjoy," he said, "you don't take music, do you?"

"I figured I was too old to start," Ratbag said gloomily.

"How old are you?"

"Fifteen."

"And how long have you been here?"

"Half a year."

"Who taught you trumpet?"

"Nobody."

Skinhead stared at him.

"Your fingering of those keys," he said, "wasn't right. But you certainly saw it *somewhere*."

"Well, I, I – " Ratbag said.

"He saw it on TV," I said.

"Which trumpet do you play?"

"No trumpet. I got no trumpet. Not me," Ratbag said. "I just – I just – "

"He picks things up," I said.

Skinhead wasn't too interested. He was just talking to let time pass because presently he said, "Now Mountjoy, a few minutes ago I played a note on that piano. Can you remember it?"

"Sure," Ratbag said.

"Play it."

Ratbag picked up the trumpet and played it.

Then he frowned and played another note, almost identical. "That's the one it *ought* to be," he said.

Skinhead had now turned very pale.

"Mountjoy," he said, "has anyone ever suggested you might have absolute pitch?"

"Absolute what?" Ratbag said.

"The ability to identify a particular note, in isolation from all others, to read the exact frequency, the wavelength of that note."

Ratbag looked puzzled.

"Can't everyone do it?" he said.

"One in a million can," Skinhead told him. "That is, one in a million can maybe *make* the note, on a trumpet, the way I just saw you do."

Ratbag stood there for a moment, quietly breathing. He looked strangely relaxed as if all of a sudden something had been put right inside him. For the first time he was looking at me – looking right at me, into my eyes.

"Hey!" he said softly. "Didn't I say it wasn't accidental? Didn't I say that? The way my notes come out?"

He didn't look crazy any more, or lost. In fact he looked as if for the first time he'd just found something out; which turned out to be right.

Boy, had he just found something out!

Three

These days you hear so much about P.V. ("Peewee") Mountjoy on radio and TV that it's incredible to think how little we knew about him at the time. We knew practically nothing. He just seemed to drift through the school like a madman. That he was in a panic most of the time, we didn't know. That he was on the run and living like a slave, we didn't know either.

Whether he saw all these things coming to him that day in the band room, I don't know. He certainly had the strangest look on his face. And he certainly had "second sight" – or so they say. He told me later he'd always felt "different", and he'd always known he was going to do something. He didn't know what it was. But he had the feeling – and so strongly at the time that he couldn't tell whether the life he was living was real or a dream or a nightmare. He'd certainly got himself in a complicated state, which I'll explain later.

For now I'll explain what we knew at the time.

We knew he wasn't quite fifteen when he first turned up at the school. We knew he'd turned up suddenly, in the middle of a term, and that the report he brought with him said he was brilliant at math. This was important because it was the one thing that got him into the school. He'd never have got in any other way, he was too much of a mess. Later on Skinhead told us that people with musical ability often were bright at math, that for some reason the two things went together. They did with Ratbag anyway; which was his good luck, for without it he wouldn't have made it or have met me or, through me, Skinhead.

That's what we knew, and it was all we knew. Except that he was a dangerous person to laugh at, and that he acted crazy and looked a freak.

Of course his own freaks now (I mean his fan clubs) describe this as his "time of searching", when he was afraid of insanity if he didn't find out the special thing about himself.

Just then in the band room he'd found it out.

And one thing more from then.

As we left the band room he was dazed and walking on air – not just stepping over rocks, his usual way, but almost lifting off as if trying to fly. His elbows were flapping, head raised, the huge brilliant eyes turning this way and that. He was gulping in air, and he said, "Hey, it was you! You know that? It was you!"

"Yeah," I said.

"You knew it? You really *felt* it there, that time?"

"Yeah, sure," I said.

What I really felt was that he ought to be at home, that he ought to be in bed. I thought he'd flipped. I thought he was having a fit.

"Right that moment I knew it! Right under that tree I knew. That you'd come for me, and it was all going to start happening. Only I felt danger too, and to do with the trumpet, so I knew I had to be careful. It's why I said what I said. But I'm sorry I said it!"

"Look, Ratbag," I told him, "we've done all that. It's OK. You've said it."

He said some other things too, but those are the ones I remember: that he'd "known" me, that he thought I'd come for him for some reason, and that there was danger with the trumpet.

Of course he was paranoid about that trumpet anyway, so you couldn't see any "second sight" there. Or I mean could you, if you wanted, sort of?

It all started happening, anyway.

Just the speed of it was amazing.

He played his first concert a month later. He still couldn't read music then. He just sat with the others and turned the pages when they turned theirs, and nobody even noticed. He was sick with fright at the time, but nobody noticed that either. Until then Skinhead hadn't been able to get him to sit with the band at all. He was too shy to turn up for rehearsals – afraid the others would laugh at his "ignorant" playing or his inability to read music.

Of course by then Skinhead had discovered his fantastic knack for memorizing the stuff. He only had to hear something once, even the most complicated piece, and he knew every note of it. That was how they managed the first concert – Skinhead lending him the cassettes, and Ratbag memorizing them. He just played his part over to Skinhead in the band room alone.

This school, of course, is very high on music, as I suppose everyone knows now – if only because of all the musical hot shots that have come from it. Franklin Lloyd Taylor, the rock opera genius, was here and Dicky Cole Bennett, the clarinettist, and Kevin "King" Cohen. Basically they play classical, but the players have spread into all kinds of music.

The strongest section has always been strings, but for some time Skinhead had been trying to beef up the wind section. The reason was financial. Government cuts had left us short of money, and one way of topping up the music fund was through prize competitions – not for the prizes themselves, which were just cups or trophies, but because certain big sponsors, banks and insurance companies, had started putting up cash to go with the prizes.

The school had always done well locally, though for years it hadn't actually won anything; so it hadn't gone through to the larger contests. Skinhead thought the reason was that our program material was too standard, so that though the playing was first-class the judges just took it for granted and handed out points to the schools playing flashier material.

To get flashy with a school orchestra meant having a good wind section, so that was his aim. And in looking through his music he'd come across a few pieces that he thought would grab the judges if only he could get the brass section right. The pieces he liked most needed first-class soloists. And the ones that could attract most attention (because they were the least played, and hardest to play) needed a number-one trumpeter.

That was the situation Ratbag blew into.

It wasn't anything special, that first concert. It was just

a school performance, to give the band an audience. You didn't even have to go to it. And hardly anybody did go. There were maybe twenty of us there. And the band fell into a shambles, and Skinhead flew into a temper, and he didn't even let them finish. And no one paid any attention to Ratbag.

I mean, Peewee. Sorry, fans.

But that was his first concert. As for the next one – wow!

It was three weeks later; by which time *everyone* was paying him attention. The news had gone round some-how – that this crazy sort of freak had got himself into the band and that there was something special about him. Nobody knew what it was, including the band; for he still hadn't turned up to rehearsals.

I won't forget it, ever.

You could hardly get in the hall, for one thing. Mainly they came to laugh – safe enough, if there are a few hundred of you and he couldn't see who was doing the laughing. I don't think he could see anything. He had the blind look again, and his face was glistening with sweat. You could just glimpse him every now and then, sitting hunched at the back with the other brass players.

For about ten minutes he didn't have to do much. Then there was a slight pause and they started a new movement; and Skinhead got them playing softer and softer until he faded them out, and pointed at Ratbag. And the most unbelievable sound came out of him.

It was a single electrifying peal. It went higher and higher. It didn't seem possible for it to go any higher.

Then it went higher, so that every hair on your head stood up. And he let it fall away and scatter into hundreds of notes, that he chased around and rounded up so that all of a sudden you realized what the band had been playing before and the whole thing came together and began to make brilliant sense.

He made brilliant sense.

He was just totally brilliant.

Nobody had ever heard anything like it, and couldn't believe it was coming from a trumpet. And even before the piece was finished everybody was up and yelling and clapping. And that was another time a school concert didn't finish. But Skinhead wasn't in a rage this time. His head was shaking in all directions, his huge mane of hair tossing about. Then he'd called Ratbag forward, and the big skinny idiot was standing there in front of the band, just looking at us.

He was dripping with sweat. It was just pouring off him. He didn't seem to know what to do with the trumpet. He was lifting it, and lowering it again; and though Skinhead was grinning away now at all the stamping and roaring that was fairly shaking the building, Ratbag wasn't. He was looking round in a kind of trance, until his eyes locked on mine and stayed there. And I had the strange feeling – that I feel now whenever I hear that song of his, "Screamin' High" – that what he'd just done he'd done for me.

And that was a funny thing, for he hadn't been near me for weeks. Since the day in the band room he hadn't said a word to me; hadn't even tried to. I thought OK, he's busy. But I felt bad about it. I thought I'd got him what he wanted so now he didn't want to know. He'd just used me.

I came out of school three days later and saw him kicking a can on the corner. He looked really strange.

He said, "Hey."

I said, "Yeah."

"You going somewhere?"

"Home."

"For something special?"

"Homework."

"Skip it."

"How's that again?" I said.

"Look, if I don't do this now," he said desperately, "I probably never will. I've been wanting to tell you. But I – it's why I kept away from you. Don't ask any questions. Just come."

"Come where? What are you – "

"Hey, man! Just come, will you?"

So I went. To his home. And I never saw anything like it.

Four

It was a big house, Victorian, four stories – five if you counted the cellar; which you had to, because they lived in it. It was the coal cellar. And the coal was still in it, piled away to one end. A wooden partition screened off the pile, but the partition only went up as far as the arch of the low roof, so you could see the coal there, and smell it. They'd whitewashed their bit but it was smudged all over with coal dust.

An electric bulb hung from the roof, but it was so dim I could barely see. I could just make out two iron beds, one each side of the cellar, and a cupboard, and a kitchen table with a couple of chairs. Apart from the gritty flagstones on the floor, that was all.

I couldn't believe anyone actually lived in the place; but they did. A girl was lying on one of the beds and she sat up as we came in. She was wearing a dressing gown, and she pulled it a bit closer when she saw me.

She was tall and skinny, like him, but a bit older, evidently his elder sister.

"I brought someone," he told her.

"You want tea now?" She just glanced at me.

"Yeah, thanks. How you feeling?" he said.

"I'm all right."

She smiled at him but didn't look at me again; and he stood a bit hunched, under the arch, waiting for her to go. Then he bolted the door behind her.

"My ma," he said.

"Your *ma*?"

He was shifting the other bed. He bent down in the space between it and the wall.

"She's pretty young," I said.

"Yeah."

He levered up a flagstone and took something out. Then he put the flagstone back and replaced the bed and unbolted the door.

"But not as young as she looks," he said. He sat at the table, nodding me to sit opposite. "She's thirty."

I worked that out. She must have been younger than he was now when he was born.

"Nice life for her here, isn't it?" he said; and that was the lousiest five minutes I ever remembered. I couldn't think what to say. He just leaned on the table and rubbed his face, looking round the cellar.

"See, she's not been well lately," he said.

"What, something – wrong?"

"No, just tired. She's had to stay home. Boy, am I going to *do* things for her!" he said fiercely. "Am I going to show her a time."

A creaky old-fashioned bell jangled suddenly, and he looked up at the ceiling.

"Wait, baby," he said to it. But he uncoiled himself after a moment and opened a door in the partition and took out two scuttles of coal. He didn't say anything and just went out with them, and I sat there and his mother came in with the tea. She didn't say anything either. She put the cups on the table and went, and presently he returned.

"Ma's in the kitchen," he said. "She has the use of that, and the bathroom. All home comforts." He sat and sipped his tea, nodding to himself.

I couldn't get over the change in him. He seemed to be in charge here, a different individual!

"See, my old lady", he said, "is one fantastic person. Only she's nervous. It's my father. That man has to be the most incredible swine living." ·

I drank my tea and wished I was somewhere else.

"A crazy old woman up there", he said casually, glancing up at the ceiling, "has us stuck here. She put a card in a window advertising for help. And my old lady fell for it. We give the help, she gives us this. All of it," he said, nodding round the cellar.

"Can't you get something – better?" I said, embarrassed.

"Yeah, I'll get a palace! I'll give it to her. I mean that," he said.

He slowly finished his tea.

"See, I do the coal. Four floors. There's lodgers here. And I clean the stairs. My old lady does the rest. And her job at the supermarket. Only she takes days off now. She's not strong. It's why I took the job there. She didn't want me to. She wants me to try a bit harder at school."

"Does she know about the – your music?"

"If you finished your tea we can go now," he said.

I drained the cup, recognizing his way of only

answering the questions he wanted to, and we went.

We went out to the back garden.

It was a big overgrown place with straggly trees and bushes. There was a flaky rose trellis three-quarters of the way down, and beyond it a mess that used to be a vegetable plot. A wooden hut stood in it, which he unlocked. "I put a new lock on this," he said, and I suddenly realized it was a key he'd taken out from under the slab.

It was dark inside and he found a box of matches and lit a storm lamp hanging on a hook. Then he closed the door and locked it from the inside.

A pile of mouldy bricks was in one corner, and he shifted it methodically and prised up a section of the floorboards underneath. There was a big tin box there, and he opened it and removed a package wrapped in a piece of blanket. In the blanket was a battered leather case, like a long attaché case. It had bits of colored tape stuck on it in the shape of a rainbow. Inside, the case was fitted with velvet-lined sections. His trumpet was there, in parts, and he briskly fitted them together and blew a few toots, experimentally.

"OK?" he said. But he didn't expect a reply and just nodded. "Yeah, it's mine. Only she doesn't know I got it. My old lady. She thinks I got rid of it. Well, I gave her the ticket."

"What ticket?"

"The pawn ticket. She's hanging on to it. She *thinks* she is. What she's got there is the ticket for the microscope."

"Microscope?"

34

"Jeeze, this is one story," he said.

He said they'd lived in some other town, where his father had been a long-distance truck driver; until the firm had kicked him out. Apparently he was a drunk, and on drugs too. He'd got some other jobs, but had kept losing them for the same reason. But whether he'd had a job or not he'd kept drinking, and also taking drugs. He got the money from Ratbag's old lady, who had a job in a factory. He beat her up for it. He beat Ratbag up too. He used to beat everybody up. They were all scared stiff of him round there.

Before he'd taken to drugs he'd been quite a nice guy. He'd played the trumpet a bit as a kid – and this was how the whole misfortune came about. In some way, on a driving job, he'd got hold of a trumpet of his own. And with a bunch of friends he'd started an amateur band. They called themselves the Rainbow Rangers and began playing in clubs and pubs. Then one night a radio producer heard them and put them on the air in a local program called "You Don't Have to be Black".

Apparently they weren't bad and they were asked again. But the producer found that Ratbag's old man was better at actually running the show – telling jokes and chatting to the listeners – than he was at playing the trumpet. So he gave him a program as a disc jockey; which turned out quite popular.

The next thing, unknown to anyone, one of the listeners taped some of the programs and sent them off to relations in the West Indies. And right out of the blue, a letter came from the radio there inviting his old man to go out and start his own show – and not just as a disc jockey but also hosting a kind of talk show. Which was how the trouble got serious.

"How?"

"See, he never worked things out. I mean he was a nice guy then – really nice. He'd give you anything. Well, he gave me the trumpet. That was when he stopped playing it and started as a disc jockey. But he wouldn't plan. He just threw up his job and took off. He said he'd send for us any day and meanwhile he'd send money ... Yeah, well he didn't," Ratbag said.

He brooded a while.

"The job didn't turn out. He was OK as a disc jockey, but he couldn't handle the people. They gave him important people to interview – politicians, big shots. And he couldn't do it, so they dropped him. And there *wasn't* any money. So apart from not sending any, he suddenly turns up again – broke. And he was a totally different guy."

Apparently he'd started on drugs before he went to the West Indies – people used to give him them in the clubs and pubs he'd played in. But with all the disappointment he had out there he'd taken to it seriously. And when he came back, he was an addict – on heroin.

He tried to get radio work again, but he couldn't, so he'd gone back to driving. And when he was slung out of that, and a few other jobs too, things went really bad. To get money for drugs he tried gambling, and to finance *that* he began selling everything they had in the house. And when Ratbag's old lady tried to stop him, he beat her up.

36

Ratbag had come home from school one day to find his old lady with a black eye and his father turning out all the drawers to find a ring he'd once given her. He knew she'd got it hidden somewhere, and he said if she didn't produce it he'd black her other eye. Ratbag had got between them and had picked up one himself.

"That was a bad scene," he said. "He was drunk, but he needed his heroin, see. He practically took the place apart, but he never found the ring. So he said OK, he'd have my trumpet instead. Except he fell asleep on the floor while he was looking for it, so we waited till he was flat out, and put a few things together, and grabbed a train and came here. The old lady has a friend here. She put us up for a couple of nights, but there was no room really, so we started looking, and saw this advert, and here we are."

"All these *months* you've been here?"

"No rent, see. We can't afford to pay any."

"But won't the welfare – "

"Well, she won't go near them! I told you, she's nervous. She's scared the old man will find us. The nearest she came to seeing any officials was when she got me in the school. This friend told her which was the best, and she'd brought my reports and everything ... She's crazy about getting me educated. She said, 'First I'll get a room for us, then a school for you, then a job for *me* so we can eat.' Which she did, all of it, and it wore her out."

He was looking gloomily at the trumpet, rubbing his fingers up and down it.

"Where does the microscope come in?" I said.

"That's what I wanted to tell you. See, I brought the trumpet here with me. And I started playing it. Only the old bat up there complained. She said it disturbed the lodgers."

"Did it?"

"Well, what do I care!" he said angrily. "Except it threw another scare into my old lady. She thought we'd get kicked out. Kicked out of here, where you're not supposed to keep a human being! Still, we had nowhere else to go. So she said, 'Look, you can't play the trumpet here so we might as well raise some money on it. We don't have to *sell* it, we can pawn it, and you'll get it back when we find somewhere else.'

"Well, I didn't want to do that," Ratbag said. "But she said, '*Please*. Do it for *me*, and I swear you'll get it back. I'll keep the pawn ticket in the Bible so you'll know.' And that's a laugh," he said. "See, she has this Bible. It's her favorite book. So I thought boy, I got to do something. I knew why she wanted the money anyway. She wanted a coat, it was getting cold. So I said, 'OK, *I'll* go to the pawnshop.' And I did."

"But not with the trumpet."

"Well, of course not with the trumpet. I wasn't going to pawn the trumpet! I'd already found a place to hide it. I found this shed. But I saw I had to raise some money fast, so I could get something to pawn. And I only knew one way of doing that. The way my old man tried. Gambling."

I stared at him.

"Yeah, I know," he said. "It sounds crazy. And it is. But he was no *good* at it. He never understood the

38

mathematics. I saw it was only a matter of figures really, and if you got them right you didn't have to risk much. He used to take risks. Anyway, I put in some extra time at the supermarket and got four pounds, and I thought I'd risk that."

Apparently he'd gone up to the library and studied the form of all the horses running in various parts of the country that week, and worked out the results of a few races.

"You can't pick a winner," he said, "not unless you're dead lucky. But if you get the figures right you can see which ones are likely to be in the first three. That's all I was going to bet on – that a particular horse would be in the first three. Of course they don't pay much for that kind of result. But you end up with more than you started with, and that goes on the second race. And so on."

"How many races *did* you bet on?"

"Three. I worked it out in the library, and went to a betting shop and wrote out the races and the horses – "

"They took a bet – from someone your age?"

"You can't tell my age," Ratbag said. Which was true, you couldn't. "So anyway, I did it, and that was it."

"The horses won?"

"No, they didn't win. I hadn't backed them to win. I just said which would be in the first three. And I had to link the bet, so if I got any one wrong I'd have lost the lot. But I didn't get them wrong. The first one came in, and paid about seven pounds, which automatically went on the next, and that came in too, which gave about thirty-two, and then the last one came up, and I ended up with ninety-four pounds."

"You're kidding!"

"Look, don't get ideas about it," Ratbag said seriously. "It's no way of making money unless you're good at numbers. I just had to do it to get something to pawn. And I already knew what that was."

"The microscope."

"Yeah. And for a reason. It was a very posh brass job. An historic instrument, it said. I'd seen it in this antique shop. Ninety quid! So I went in and bought it, and took it right to the pawnshop. I showed them the receipt, and they gave me forty pounds for it. Forty quid for a ninety-pound microscope! Still, you get a ticket for it so you can always get it back if you keep up the commission payments. And I was only interested in the ticket anyway, and what they'd write on it. So I said OK, forty quid, and took it."

"What did they write on it?"

"That was the point of the microscope. I told them to put 'brass instrument' – which could cover a trumpet too, see. My old lady never questioned it anyway. And she did put it in the Bible. Which is another joke," he said. "She found a place where it says 'The trumpet shall sound.' And that's where she keeps it. That's really a joke, isn't it?"

"Yeah," I said, but he didn't laugh so I didn't either. He was taking the trumpet apart and putting it back in the case again.

"You're the only one that knows this," he said. "I been wanting to tell you. Boy, I was scared when you found me with it that day! I thought if she learned I still had the trumpet – which she might if there'd been any trouble – she'd be hurt. I mean *really* hurt, not just a black eye. And I'm not having that. I'm not having her hurt any more! So I got a problem. I got problems here," he said.

He'd closed the case and was fingering the bits of colored plastic on it. "The Rainbow Rangers," he said. "They weren't too good really. My old man wasn't, either. He gave me a few lessons, but I knew it wasn't right the way he showed me."

"Well, you've got it right now," I said.

He grunted. "How you think I was the other night?"

"You know how you were. You were great."

"No I wasn't."

He was moodily rubbing the plastic.

"But I might *get* great with this one. It's what I started with. I got a feeling for it. My old man said a funny thing when he gave me it. He said, 'There's a pot of gold for you at the end of this rainbow, Paulie.' He used to call me Paulie. 'You got a tongue,' he said."

"A tongue?"

"It's what they said of the old black musicians, the great ones. That they had a tongue. See, with a trumpet it's fingers and tongue. The fingers you learn. But the tongue is natural, if you got it. I thought he was just saying it. But then last week Skinhead said it too. And with the *band* trumpet, that I don't feel anything for … This one – remember you said it laughed and cried?"

"It did."

"Well, the band trumpet won't! I can't make it. It's this. It wasn't new when my old man got it. It was second-hand, third-hand, maybe even fourth. It's old.

And black musicians have always played it … Yeah, with this one I could get great. Maybe. I think."

"And that's the problem?"

"Yeah!"

I didn't go back in the coal cellar. I went home. I thought about him all the way.

Five

I saw Skinhead two days later. I saw him confidentially. I said if he didn't want to do it, Ratbag must never know.

"Know what?" he said.

So I told him a version. I told him Ratbag knew of a trumpet that had belonged to a black guy, and he thought he could play better with it. And he wanted to have it.

"How can I help?" Skinhead said.

"By writing to his mother."

"Saying what?"

"That the school wants to *make* the trumpet available to him."

"We haven't any money."

"It won't cost any," I said.

"But if it won't – "

"Something like this," I said, and showed him the letter I'd scribbled. "Written by *you*, sir. On school paper."

He read the letter and looked at me.

"We can do this without money?" he said.

"I guarantee it."

"Well, I don't know," he said.

"He's a marvel with that trumpet, sir!"

"Is he?"

"A marvel. He can do anything with it."

"Hm," he said, and I knew he was hooked. He didn't understand it, and it might take time, but he'd do it.

Which he did, and I gave Ratbag the letter and watched him read it, knowing he could either thank me or just start taking me apart: there was no way of knowing with him.

He didn't thank me. He didn't take me apart either, though. He just looked at me and read it again.

"What's this supposed to do?" he said.

"Get you the trumpet."

He worked that one out.

"But it's lies – all of it."

"Yeah? Pick one out."

He read the letter a third time, and I knew it so well I could almost read it with him.

Dear Mrs Mountjoy,

As Paul's music teacher I would like to express my great satisfaction at his progress with the school orchestra. I understand he has experience with a trumpet that he prefers to the school instruments. I would appreciate it if you would allow me, on behalf of the school, to assist in making this trumpet available to him – of course at no cost to yourself.

Yours sincerely ...

"How can the *school* make it available?" he said. "You know it's just lies. It's conning her."

"The way you've been doing?"

He didn't say anything. He just looked at me, and took off, and I didn't see him again for a couple of days. But when I did he had the trumpet with him; and the pawn ticket for the microscope was where the trumpet used to be: locked up in the shed.

I'd worked it out, and he had too. He'd told his old lady the school was paying to get the trumpet out of pawn, so could he have the pawn ticket? So that's how we managed it, and it cost nothing.

And as his mother's favorite book promised, the trumpet began to sound. And how it sounded!

They were doing the locals just then, and Skinhead and the band sailed through them. They'd never had trouble with local contests, and they didn't this time. They won the lot, and he didn't even use Ratbag much. He was saving him for the serious rounds.

The first serious one was the county championship, and even then he didn't overwork him. He mainly drilled the band; and though Ratbag had the occasional solo, the new pieces he'd chosen depended more on skillful playing by the band as a whole.

So we got that in the bag too, and were county champions. And now the going got tough. Now there were the regionals, and we'd never won those before – not even in the school's best days.

For the regionals they divided the country into four – north, south, east and west – and the county champions played each other to decide who was king of the region. And now Skinhead began to sweat. He'd been scooting round the country listening to the other bands, and he

45

knew what we were up against. They were all good, very good; and their brass sections were a knockout.

His problem was that he was scared to use Ratbag too early. He knew he could be great; but also that he was nervous, with no experience of big audiences. Also, in the pieces that showed him off best the rest of the brass section couldn't support him. They weren't good enough yet.

(I didn't hear this from Ratbag. I don't know if he even knew it. I got it from Sammy, the kid with the flute, who knew everything. I'll tell about him later.)

So, for a start, Skinhead began drilling the brass section. He drilled them like a maniac. He threatened them and he begged them. He almost went down on his knees to them. He gave them double rehearsal periods. He played them cassettes. He had them in one at a time and corrected their playing. Then he had sets of them in and corrected them as sets. Then he had the whole band, and had them playing the tricky bits five, ten, twenty times. They were nervous wrecks before the first concert.

But boy, they were different! Even I could tell the difference. The strings came in like one instrument. The trombones rasped in and practically blew you out of your seat. And over the top came Ratbag, high and clear, pulling them all together as he had before.

We went storming round the region and knocked them cold. We just bombed them out one after the other. Even the local papers noticed. First they noticed the busloads from our school (for Ratbag had become a kind of mascot now, and hundreds who knew nothing about music had started following him). Then they noticed Ratbag himself.

Skinhead had told him to close his eyes when he played his solos so that the audiences wouldn't scare him. And that was the weirdest sight. He came snaking out of his seat and stood there swaying, eyes tight shut, playing like a dream.

The whole thing was like a dream. As he gained in confidence, the whole band became confident. They were more or less unstoppable. And that was in the bag, too – the regional championship! And the strangest thing happened with Skinhead. Before, he'd set his sights only on this. A good cash prize came with it, which we'd never had before; so he'd achieved what he wanted. But not any more. Now he had another idea. He had the idea we were going to be the *national* champions.

And actually this wasn't so crazy. For each year's nationals a different panel of judges was chosen; and this year's, as he'd already found out, were all mad about brass. It even went further. The chief adjudicator for the finals, specially flying in for the occasion, was to be Julius van Bergh. He was a trumpeter himself – apparently the world's greatest – and he was judging all the nationals. The international, next year, was to be held in his own city, Amsterdam.

That was the situation, anyway, and the whole giddy round started again. Regional play-offs: east against west, north against south. Semi-finals. Finals. And we were there. And van Bergh was there. And photographers were there. And three hundred of our lot were pouring out of buses. And that was another night no one will forget.

It wasn't really ever in doubt. The others played off first, and they were good, tremendously good. They still didn't have a chance. Skinhead had picked two pieces, and the first we'd played before, as had several other bands in the contest. But this time, with the improved brass section, we roared away with it. Skinhead had almost hypnotized them into total confidence. Also, they knew what was coming. It was his second piece that was the masterstroke: a modern concerto for trumpet and full orchestra. Which *nobody* had played before during the entire contest. Hardly anyone had played it anyway, it was so difficult. But one person in that hall had played it. Van Bergh had. Was famous for it. And for the past month the band had been driven crazy listening to him on tape.

Either you like that kind of music or you don't. Normally I can hardly stand it. But this time was different. This time Ratbag was playing it. And again, right on cue, he came snaking out of his seat, eyes tight shut, the totally weird music pouring out of him. He played half notes and double notes. He sent long processions of little stuttering notes echoing round the ceiling, then scooped them off the floor and fed them back to the band. He stopped abruptly in the middle of a passage, and complete silence fell on the hall; and stood there, eyes tight shut, waiting, till he suddenly started again with a long mocking bray that seemed to ask what everyone was waiting for.

I'd heard it before, I didn't like it before, and I still

48

didn't like it. But you couldn't stop listening; you couldn't stop looking. He was totally fantastic. And long before he'd finished I saw van Bergh's mouth had dropped open, and he was making little jerky movements of his head at the exact moment Ratbag had to come in again. Skinhead was making the same movements. He was working like a madman with the band, seeing they all came in on time. And boy, they did. They didn't miss a thing. And after the long last pause, when the audience wasn't sure if it had finished or not – and then saw Ratbag abruptly sit down, and realized it had, the roaring started.

That roaring!

And the photographers were there, flashing off at Ratbag. And the judges had their heads together, as if there was something to decide. Then the announcement. Then Ratbag, standing in a trance again, having his hand shaken by van Bergh. More photographs. The trophy. And we were on the long ride back, with every-one talking about Amsterdam.

So that's the background, and the reason we got in such a fix. I mean the story's hardly started yet so if any of that sounded wild – better prepare for take-off. I mean fasten seat-belts, OK?

Six

It's maybe the craziest city in the world, Amsterdam. It's only small but there are a thousand bridges in it, and 160 canals, and water everywhere. And cobbled lanes between the water, with millions of bikes wobbling about, and pairs of linked-up trams clanging between them. And here we came, nudging along in our two buses, bombed out after the drive, and starving hungry.

We'd crossed the Channel and driven through France and Belgium. We'd eaten every Mars bar and Malteser in sight. There wasn't a can of Coke left. It was nearly ten at night, and the floodlights were on everywhere. We went jostling through all the honking and hooting and finally pulled up at the hostel; and five minutes later were stuck into a warmed-up meal.

An exhausting day – in fact an exhausting week! One of the buses was for the band, all expenses paid, and the other for the supporters – no expenses paid. Some of the kids hadn't managed to get the money together till a couple of days before. One kid hadn't made it till the *day* before. Sammy, the kid with the flute who mixed himself up with everything, had gone up to the travel agents with him to see that he got on at all.

One reason for all the last-minute flap was that our

performance date had been changed. The play-off took two days, and we'd been listed to play the second one. Then one of the foreign bands had trouble, so they'd switched *us*: to the first day.

That's how it was. That's how we landed in it. But we were here now. And next day was play-off.

So many things happened those last few months, I've left a few out.

The whole contest – locals, counties, regionals, nationals – had been going on in all twelve competing countries since the autumn. It had been going on through winter and spring; and now it was summer. It was July. And in Amsterdam it was the middle of the Holland Festival; which was how it had been planned. The school international was one of the events of the Festival. And the city was crowded, bursting at the seams, every room booked up.

In this period, things had changed drastically for Ratbag. His whole life had changed. No more coal cellar. They were in a proper flat now – with Skinhead and the school office fixing the whole thing. Welfare was paying the rent (with every kind of assurance that Ratbag's old man wouldn't be contacted in any way) and there was no more cleaning, and no more coal scuttles.

Also, instead of being a half-crazy freak with no friends he now had hundreds of friends – at least people who wanted to be friends with him. But this was a way he hadn't changed. He was still a loner, still very moody, and still half crazy! He wouldn't give up the idea that

I'd been "sent" to him; that we were bound together in some way, and that I had to be there when he played. He still wore his little woolly hat and the two odd sneakers – his lucky ones, he said. He'd brought them with him, as well as his lucky trumpet.

Then there was Sammy – who was mainly responsible for what followed. He's a very little kid, Sammy, almost a midget, with big glasses. His hobby's bird-watching. He'd tagged along after me for years; had been doing it all during these months; had been the one to tell me how the band was doing, and of Ratbag's progress. He sees a lot, and remembers a lot, which is one of the troubles with him. And it was the trouble this time.

The play-off was at the Concertgebouw, headquarters of the Amsterdam symphony orchestra. *Gebouw* means "building", and this one was a cracker – 2,200 seats and the best acoustics in Europe. Three bands played the morning session and three the afternoon. We had the afternoon, but we went along in the morning all the same. And Skinhead was gloomy right away. A Danish band kicked off, and they were terrific. Then a German one, ditto. Then one from Holland itself, even more ditto. And Skinhead's spirits sank and sank. The whole band's did. They'd never had to play up to this level before, and they knew it.

He gave them a pep talk during lunch: said we still had the best program material – the trumpet concerto again. And that though van Bergh wasn't here this time (he was playing concerts in America), this might actually work to our advantage. Van Bergh had *heard* us do it, but these guys hadn't, and just the novelty of it would knock them over. Also, none of the opposition had anyone like Ratbag.

So we went in, and had to listen to the Russians (a fantastic performance, hand-picked every one of them). Then we were on ourselves. And I could see every kid in the band was white and trembling. The whole audience could see it – every seat in the hall taken. And Skinhead had his baton up, and his huge head of hair shook, and they were off.

That they were brilliant was never in doubt. They were *unbelievable*. They'd never done better – ever. They stormed away, and Ratbag picked up his cue dead on time, and weirdly swayed there as he had done before, the music pouring out of him. And again, his identical performance – the abrupt pause, him standing there, eyes tight shut, the dead silence in the hall, then the long mocking bray that broke it. And it was over, and Skinhead's arms had dropped, and Ratbag had sat down. And the roaring started.

That roaring again!

But we couldn't tell. They were marking each performance as it finished; marking very closely, to a tenth of a point. And the Russians were clear ahead, two whole points ahead. There was no hope of catching *them*, we knew that. But we were after a place; to be in the first three. No British band had done that before. And then our marks were announced; and the roaring again! We'd beaten the Danes, the Germans, the Dutch. We were second to the Russians – a point and a half behind, with another band to play today and six more tomorrow. But second for the time being ... A fantastic achievement for a band that had never made it to Europe before.

Then the French came on, demoralized after our performance, and tried their best, and it wasn't good enough; and they left demoralized. And everything packed up for the day, with the various bands trying to figure out where they stood. Except for the Russians, who knew, and were hugging each other. We were pretty high, too. We went off on a tour.

We'd booked the tour before we left, and we took it by boat.

Though there are 160 canals, there are only four main ones; they're parallel with each other in a ring round the port, so if you carry on long enough you keep turning up at the place you started from. There are dozens of little cuttings linking the canals, and the guide gave us the story as we drifted through.

We heard about the two men and the dog who were out fishing one day over a thousand years ago and got caught in a storm and took refuge on a sandbank at the mouth of the Amstel river. And how they thought it was a useful place to be, less waterlogged than the rest of the lowlands, and brought their families over and built a village. And how they raised the sandbank so that high tides wouldn't wash away what they'd built. And how this was the first dam on the Amstel, or the Amstel dam, which became Amsterdam. Which was a useful illustration, the guide said, of how the dog really was man's best friend and helped to found the Dutch empire.

Sammy couldn't see what was so good about an empire or even where the dog came in, and kept asking, and the guide grew angry and said it probably swam ashore first, and to shut up.

Anyway, the Amsterdamers got a charter to the place 700 years back which exempted them from paying taxes on any goods they landed. And those guys started landing goods! With a safe anchorage they picked up half the trade of Europe. They started buying and selling the goods. Then when the Portuguese found a route to India and began shipping goods back, the Amsterdamers went to Portugal and bought them, to sell to the rest of Europe.

Until they decided to cut the Portuguese out and get the stuff themselves; which meant building a merchant fleet to do it. And warships to protect the fleet. And a force of fighting men for the warships and the military bases they needed. Which was how the empire came about.

Because the ships had to sail so far, they needed a half-way post for food and medical supplies; which was the beginning of Cape Town and the colonization of Africa. And as they sailed farther still, finding newer routes, they found more places. They found Fiji and New Zealand and Australia – 150 years before Captain Cook.

And it even went beyond that. Because the profits were so fantastic – they were bringing back silk and spices and jewels and tea – other countries began getting in on the act. To keep ahead, the Amsterdamers had to cut prices; which meant cutting their expenses. The main expense was the number of days the ships spent at sea; so if they found shorter routes they could cut their costs. By this time they knew the world was round, so they figured that to get to the far east it could be quicker to go west. They sent a captain west, Henry Hudson, to see if he could hit China that way.

He didn't hit China but he hit somewhere else and sailed up a river (which he named for himself, the Hudson river); and found an island which he called New Amsterdam – and which the British later took and called New York. So we heard all that, and the guide kept droning on.

He'd begun pointing out mansions now; which was another thing. The canals were lined with mansions, all jammed tightly together. They were the homes of the merchants who'd grown so rich about the time Hudson was looking for China in New York harbor, and most of them had sixteen hundred and something carved on them. They were very narrow and tall, several stories tall; with all the stories highly decorated to show how rich their owners had been.

They'd ordered fancy gables and coats of arms, and colored sculptures to illustrate the trades they'd been engaged in. And at the top they had poles sticking out – hoists for pulling up the goods their ships brought from the east. The attics had been jammed with their goods. And not only the attics. Because the houses were packed so close together they had little space to show off their more personal possessions. But pictures didn't need much space, so they competed to buy them – by the hundred, by the thousand – and the Dutch school of painting came about, Rembrandt, Vermeer, Steen, Hals ...

My eyes had started closing with this floating history lesson, and so had most of the others'. But not Sammy's. He stayed awake. Mansions kept going past, and Sammy kept watching them ...

We were up early next morning, and in the concert hall early. And were hammered early.

Right off, a bunch of Hungarians took the stage and knocked us into third place. Then two more bands followed and left the situation that way – Russians first, Hungarians second, British third – with three bands still to come in the afternoon session. And we went off to lunch.

I didn't eat much lunch. Hardly anyone else ate theirs either. Sammy ate all his. He ate half someone else's too. He was always hungry, that kid. And we went back in again ...

For the Italians to knock us into fourth place, and the Czechs into fifth; so we came nowhere. It was disappointing certainly, after holding second place for the first day. But a thousand times better than anyone dared hope back in the autumn! And there was no doubt who was the star of the show. Photos of Ratbag and his trumpet were in all the papers.

We talked about it, and talked about it, and couldn't talk of anything else. We talked right through tea. Then Sammy looked at his watch and said, "Well, sixteen hours to go." (We were off at ten in the morning.) "How about getting our money's worth in this place?"

He was looking at me, and I looked at Ratbag.

"How about it?" I said.

"Yeah, why not?" He was smiling. He was pretty cheerful then. "Sure," he said. "Let's go."

Which we did; and that's how the trouble started for us.

Seven

I think we heard of the place in a "What's On" guide they had in the hostel. It was an area with streets of little cafés where musicians played Dixieland jazz. We got a tram outside the hostel and jumped off as we passed the lights: three of us, Ratbag, Sammy and me.

The tram took us too far and we had to walk back (which was useful later when we tried to work out where it had happened). We passed a floating flower market with boats tied together and plants and buckets of flowers spread over on to the canalside. And several little bridges and bits of canal. And Sammy remembered seeing a couple of signs he thought said Prince's Craft and Singer (which turned out to be Prinsengracht and Singel). None of it meant much at the time: we were just heading back to the cafés.

The streets we wanted were off a square called the Leidseplein (*plein* means square), we knew that much. And for some time we just wandered about them, trying to work out which cafés were cheapest. And Sammy grew hungry again, and started complaining that they still owed us a supper at the hostel and maybe we should have waited till we'd had it. He hadn't spent a penny so far the whole trip, and he didn't plan to spend much tonight either. He was hanging on to his money for a pair of duty-free binoculars he wanted on the way back, for bird-watching.

It wasn't dark yet, though electric bulbs were flashing round the cafés, but all of a sudden floodlighting lit up the canals, and Ratbag said, "Hey, we going to wander here all night?" and he picked the next place and walked right in without giving Sammy a chance to check the prices. It was a popular place, very lively – and so crowded we were turned away from the main room and shown to a table on a glassed-in veranda outside. We'd already walked through it, trying to get in.

You could see the band and hear the music there, so we didn't mind; except there were no menus and Sammy nearly went out of his mind trying to find one. And when the waiter came he played safe and just ordered a glass of lemonade, while Ratbag and I had Coke and some kind of cake everybody was eating.

It was very noisy and smoky, the air thick with the little cigars everyone seemed to be smoking. The whole place was jumping, and Ratbag knew all the numbers the band played and sat there swaying and wriggling his shoulders in that strange way of his. Then the next thing, we heard a commotion outside and looked out the window and saw a little open car driving straight along the pavement. (The street was so narrow, cars weren't supposed to enter it.) And that car was a sight. There were maybe ten people in it, all tangled together and hanging over the side, and they came pouring out and into the café, laughing and pushing each other. They were a bit older than us – I figured university students, which turned out to be right.

A girl had been driving, and she was the one to spot Ratbag.

What happened next I'm not absolutely sure, but in some way we'd been scooped out of the veranda and were inside with them. It was still full in there, jam-packed, and even noisier and smokier; but they seemed to be regulars and waiters started running everywhere. They were shifting people about and moving tables, and in no time we were all crowded round a couple of shoved-together tables and drinking something a bit peculiar.

(To be on the safe side, and in case he was asked to buy another drink, Sammy had brought his lemonade with him; but he drank the new stuff too.)

We weren't paying for it and I couldn't tell what it was (something sweetish like coconut and pineapple but stronger), and anyway there was such confusion we didn't even ask. They were speaking Dutch among themselves and English to us, and it turned out they'd recognized Ratbag not only from the papers but because some of them had been in the hall when he played. And they were crazy about him!

We couldn't understand half what they said – we were sitting right under the band – but then members of the band got involved too, and it was plain what they wanted. And Ratbag was up on his feet, protesting and saying, "Hey, man, hey!" and four of them were helping him, and he was standing up there with a trumpet in his hand, scowling and grinning in turn. And the band had struck up "When the Saints Go Marching In", and he was playing it.

Boy!

He was like fifty times better than the band! I'd never heard him do this stuff before. I didn't know he *could* do it. (Skinhead had lent him cassettes of all the jazz classics to help with his "tongueing", but he hadn't mentioned it. He hadn't mentioned anything about his training: always secretive.) And he started belting out different styles. He gave them six or seven – Louis Armstrong and Miles Davis and Dizzy Gillespie, and people I'd never heard of. After the first one he said which way he was going to play, and then played it.

And I don't know what happened to him there! I'd seen it before, the amazing change that could suddenly come over him – I'd seen it in the coal cellar and I'd seen it in the concerts. But I still couldn't explain it. He seemed to take on an atmosphere and dominate it. He still kept his eyes tight shut when he played, but he was totally unselfconscious. He played and he played. He gave them "Basin Street Blues" and "Groovin' High" and "I Got Rhythm" and several others; and when the band couldn't follow, he did it on his own and the whole café watched him open-mouthed. Then at some point somebody called out, "Sing it! Sing it!" and everyone else took it up.

He didn't want to. Said he couldn't. That he never had; but inside half a minute the band's singer, who was also the guitarist, had produced a sheet with words, and Ratbag had started on the "St Louis Blues".

(So that was the first time his strange husky croak was heard in public: all on that same incredible night …)

He started slowly, a bit hesitantly, peering at the words in the dim light. But whatever he did he couldn't go wrong! The hesitation sounded like real feeling, like pain, as if he was groping hard for words to express himself. And I never heard it sung like that before; and from the row they made nobody else did either.

They went wild; they went crazy. They were shrieking and whooping and banging tables, and everyone on the veranda had come crowding in too; and I could see people staring in from outside. They wouldn't let him go. Everything he'd played before he had to sing now; and he started varying it, playing a bit and singing a bit, till he was really croaking and had to stop and come down. And he was so dry he drank a glass straight off without stopping.

We'd had another of these drinks while he played, and we had one more when he joined us. Sammy had been nervous of it but the waiter told him it wouldn't hurt a baby. (Some baby! There was white rum in those drinks which we couldn't taste because of the coconut and pineapple; and poor Sammy was drunk without knowing it. He hadn't even had the slice of cake we'd had, which had helped to absorb it.)

After a while I felt my head start to spin, and saw Sammy looking very white; then we seemed to be outside. And the floating flower market was going past, and floodlights and glittering water, and I was mixed up with arms and legs in an open car. Then we were out of it and staggering about on a pavement, and Ratbag was laughing his head off and pointing something out to me; and I remembered he'd had two more glasses before we left – people had come up and bought them for him.

Then we weren't in the street any more but in a house,

a huge tall one, and going up flights of stairs. And we were in a room, a very long one, richly furnished, with spotlit pictures on the walls and the kind of furniture I'd only seen before on films or television. And I was sunk into a sofa, eating a plate of open sandwiches. There was smoked salmon and caviare (I remember someone saying it) and champagne corks were popping. I don't think I drank any but I remember Ratbag did. He always seemed to have a glass in his hand, and he was singing. They'd put records on and he was singing to them.

Then I was being shown round – not Ratbag, not Sammy, just me and four or five students. There was a Nellie and a Saskia, and a Max and Danny and Jan. And we'd gone up another flight of stairs and were in an attic, quite a big one, though apparently only a part of all the floor space up there.

The attic was a kind of museum: there were old things in it, barrels and chests, with a collection of antique tools on the wall. And no windows but a sort of double-door where the window should be. I remember there was some commotion getting this open because of a tricky system of bolts. But they managed it and we looked out, and someone hung on to me as I peered down and saw a narrow slice of canal winking far below, with a barge moored opposite.

The buildings on the other side of the water, a whole terrace of them, had the same kind of wooden shutters on every story, like warehouses. And I remember noticing a pole sticking out right above us, and realizing just at the same moment that I must be in one of the mansions the guide had pointed out during the trip.

Also, something we hadn't been able to see from water level, there was a hook on the end of it, and a rope strung tight along the pole and entering the attic through a hole above the shutter.

There was a lot of laughing as they tried to unwind the rope, which I knew they weren't supposed to, it was historic; and they couldn't anyway. It was attached to a kind of winch with a small handle on it, and the whole thing was fixed to the wall beside a framed notice in Dutch that apparently explained its history.

Then the next thing we were back in the main room, and Ratbag was still singing. More people seemed to have arrived, some of them much older, and one of them quite old. I had the idea he was the owner of the place, maybe the father of the girl who'd brought us. He seemed quite amiable, not objecting to the row or the fact that a party was going on. Then I spotted Sammy, looking very white and shaky, going out the door, and I went over to see if he was all right. But I got held up on the way, people talking to me, and before I could leave he was back.

I went to him and said, "You OK, Sammy?"

"I think so. Yes. I think so." He was looking better, but puzzled. "Where are we?" he said.

"I don't know. But it must be getting late."

He looked at his watch and said, "Late? – It's five to eleven. They shut that place at ten!"

I went over to Ratbag fast, but actually needn't have bothered. People had been coming and going all the time, and I saw a guy come in then, in a hurry. He had a word with the older man, who seemed to blow a fuse. He

65

started waving his arms and snapping at people, apparently telling them the party was over and to beat it. And in no time we were all downstairs again.

The girl seemed to know our problem about getting back, because the next thing we were in her car and jetting along fast between the canals. Then she was waving goodbye and we were bashing on the door; and having an argument with a grumpy old guy on the other side who'd locked it ...

Which, even then, wasn't quite all for the night.

Skinhead was waiting for us, rather pale.

"There's been a call for you, Mountjoy," he said. "From Julius van Bergh, in New York. He's heard the reports. He wants to see you next month. In Amsterdam."

"Amsterdam?" Ratbag said. He didn't seem to realize he was there already. He was having trouble focusing. "What for?"

"To consider you for a scholarship. To his master class."

"Is that good?" Ratbag said.

"Good? It's beyond price," Skinhead said. "If he takes you, you're made for life. Only think of the honor for the school! I tell you, Mountjoy, my head is still spinning."

His wasn't the only one.

As we turned in Sammy said to me, "Was I sick tonight?"

"I don't know. Maybe."

"I think I was," he said. "Yes. In a bathroom."

"OK, get your head down now."

"That was a strange thing," he said curiously.

"Yeah, good night."

"Very strange," he said, and went rabbiting on, but I didn't listen. I could hear Ratbag already snoring away. He hadn't taken in his special news yet. There was a lot we hadn't taken in tonight, and it was still going on. It was all going on out there and waiting for us, next day.

Eight

We had thick heads next day, and everything seemed too loud. Breakfast was at eight, and we had to have all our gear packed and lined up by nine. We'd had this business on the way out: all the band's instruments had to be checked by Skinhead, with everyone standing by his own. They were to go in a special locked compartment in the side of the bus, and Skinhead signed a Customs declaration to say what they were. Our own bags just went in the boot at the back.

Ratbag kept licking his lips and drinking gallons of water. He was only slowly coming to and realizing what Skinhead had told him. I was slowly coming to myself. And so was Sammy. He still had the puzzled look and was wandering about the hall, scratching his head. He was doing it when the courier turned up.

We'd had this guy, with an assistant, at the other end before we left. He had a different assistant this time, but it was the same routine. He called out names and ticked everyone off while his side-kick checked the luggage. It took a bit of time but presently we were off and nudging our way through Amsterdam again. And the same journey, but in reverse: through Holland to the Belgian frontier, then through Belgium to the border with

France. By three-thirty we were at Calais, with Sammy first off the band's bus and rushing into the duty-free shop for his binoculars.

Several of us joined him there and saw him drive the sales staff mad finding what he wanted. He knew exactly what it was, a pair of Japanese ones that he had a pamphlet for; and knew the price of. They couldn't lay hands on them at first and kept showing him other kinds, more expensive, but he kept on – practically till the hovercraft was ready to go. In the end he got them, and steamed aboard with Skinhead yelling at him and the courier almost having a fit.

We'd taken the hovercraft, coming over, and there was nothing to it. The buses drove right on and parked in the car bay, while we went to the cabin. It was very crowded, and we just had time to jam ourselves in, and for the stewardesses to struggle round giving out drinks, and we were at Dover – half an hour. The craft went shuttling there and back all day.

Then we were assembled in the Customs shed, and Skinhead and the Customs guy were counting the cases in the hold, and we were on the road again. And twenty miles out of Dover we stopped for "rest room activities", as Skinhead put it. We'd done the same on the way out. They had a motorway service station there.

By this time everyone was starving again – we'd only had packed lunches on the buses – so we all lined up at the self-service counter upstairs. Except Sammy, who was broke. I bought him a Coke and a bun anyway, and was just bringing the tray back when I saw him hopping about at the window and yelling. Before I'd put the tray down he was gone – taking the stairs three at a time.

I went to the window and looked out, and saw him running out into the forecourt. He began dashing round and round the two buses, and presently the drivers, who were having a cigarette with the courier some distance away, went over to see what he was doing.

Several people were at the window by this time, so I got them to watch my tray and went down myself. Skinhead was there when I arrived, and Sammy was babbling that someone had pinched a case from the bus. They began inspecting the bus, the band's bus – Skinhead, Sammy, the courier and the two drivers. They inspected the locked compartment in the side. Skinhead and the courier tried the compartment and found it still locked.

"You imagined it, boy," Skinhead said.

"No, sir, I didn't, sir. Honest, sir. I *saw* him – through these!" Sammy yelled. He had his new binoculars dangling round his neck. "I was trying them out, and I looked at the bus, and there he was. He'd got the case out and was just locking the door. I think he went off in a car, but I'm not sure. I just came dashing down."

"Well," Skinhead said, a bit dubiously, "we'd better check," and he got out his key. He was the only one to have a key because of the declaration he'd signed.

The driver of the bus began humping the stuff out, a bit surly at the extra work, and Skinhead and the courier checked it against the list. There was nothing missing so in the end it all went back in, and Skinhead told Sammy to take a rest. "It's been a long day ... now go on," he said when Sammy started babbling again. "Cut along, before I lose my temper!" And the rest of the band saw

70

he did, grabbing him by the collar, because the drivers, grumbling at the delay, were already climbing back in.

So I never ate what I'd paid for upstairs, and within a couple of minutes we were on the road again. And I didn't see any of the band till we got to the other end. Even then I didn't see much of them. Their bus had taken off first, the driver, still ticked off with having to hump luggage, roaring away so that we lost them in the suburbs.

They'd been in some time when we arrived, and both Ratbag and Sammy had gone. Almost everybody had gone.

I went home myself, tired.

I'd been in about an hour when Ratbag phoned.

He said, "Can you get here?" He sounded strange.

"I'm tired, I'm going to bed. What is it?"

"Get here, I'll show you," he said, and hung up.

I looked at the phone and cursed.

I went, though. I went to the new flat. It was on the second floor of a house and I hadn't seen it before. It was pretty bare there, no real furniture; but better than a coal cellar.

His mother was in the living-room watching a black and white TV. She didn't look round and he didn't take me in there. He unlocked his bedroom and switched the light on. Then he locked the door again. He had the curtains drawn. His trumpet case was lying on the bed, and he opened it. "This ain't my trumpet," he said.

I looked at him, then at the trumpet. It was in the case. I flipped the lid and saw the plastic rainbow.

"What are you talking about?" I said.

"It's not mine. The case ain't, either."

"Are you sure?"

"Hey, you think I'm crazy? I tell you this lot's not mine. I thought it didn't feel right when I picked it up," he said. "It was heavier. Now I know it ain't."

I thought of Sammy's story.

"What do you think happened?"

"I don't *know* what happened. But I packed mine this morning, and this isn't it."

I looked at the label on the handle.

"The handwriting's yours."

"The writing's mine, the label's mine, the rest isn't."

"Hang on," I said, seeing his hysterical eyes. I began reasoning it out. "You packed it this morning, and then what?"

"I put it on the counter. With the other stuff."

"And waited while Skinhead checked it off."

"Sure."

"And put it on the bus."

"No. I didn't. A guy put it on. That guy did."

"You saw him."

"Yeah. Well, I think so."

"Ratbag," I said. "You weren't bright this morning."

"No." He licked his lips. "What's going on here?" he said.

We looked at each other.

"You *knew* the case was heavier when you picked it up?"

"Yeah, only I was tired. I thought that's all it was. So I came home and dumped it and had tea. Then came

72

back in here again and it *was* heavier. So I took the trumpet out and that was OK, though it didn't seem to be mine. It's the case. Feel it." He closed the case and hefted it himself before giving it to me.

I didn't know how it was supposed to feel anyway, so I said, "We'd better get Skinhead."

I went down to the coin box in the hall and phoned him. He was tired himself and said couldn't it wait till the morning. But he seemed to catch something in my voice and said OK, he'd be over, and I went back up again.

Ratbag was fiddling with the case.

He said, "This is some copy! Look at the scratches and the thumps. And the rainbow and the label and everything. Even the interior. Except the velvet's more scuffed in mine. Boy, this could fool me."

"Why would anyone want to fool you?"

"Yeah, why would they?" he said.

"Is the trumpet any good?"

He put it together and blew a few toots.

"Yeah, it's OK."

"I mean, is yours a better one? Could that be a reason for anyone switching it?"

"No way."

"It's the case, then," I said, and picked it up with both hands and weighed it. It did seem heavy for an empty case. He watched me a moment and went to a box in the corner. He came back with a screwdriver. He got down on his knees and started picking at the inside of the case, prising the velvet up all round, and carefully tugging. The whole thing came out – all the shaped velvet interior, like a cutlery tray. There was a layer of protective padding underneath in little bags, like plastic foam. Except it wasn't. He prodded a bag with his finger, and the stuff inside moved like salt.

"What is it – anti-damp compound?" I said.

He gave me a funny look.

"No way, bub. Anti-people," he said. "I seen this stuff before. I seen my old man use it. It's heroin."

That was about half past eight; and by half past nine we had it worked out, sort of.

Nine

We were in the police station – Ratbag, Skinhead, myself and Sammy. Skinhead had sent for Sammy, and he still wasn't fully awake. He'd gone to bed as soon as he'd got in.

The CID men were taking him there and back through his story of someone pinching a case from the bus, when he suddenly started blinking and scratching his head again.

"Wait a minute," he said. "Something happened earlier. I knew I hadn't imagined it. Like being sick last night. Remember I asked you about it?" he said to me. "*Was* it only last night?"

"Yeah," I said, and explained about him being sick, but the police weren't interested and asked what he meant about something happening earlier.

He said, "Well, I wasn't feeling too terrific this morning. And I was trying to remember where I was sick when the courier turned up and started doing the luggage. Well, his assistant did. And I thought, oh no, I can't be seeing things again. I thought I'd been seeing things when I was sick. And I thought I'd seen this guy before, too, the assistant, which seemed impossible – he hadn't *been* with us before. It was another one. So I watched him pretty closely, and I saw him change Ratbag's case!"

"Whose case?" the chief detective said. He was a plain-clothes inspector.

"Ratbag's. Mountjoy's. He took it off the trolley and put another one there in its place."

The detective got Skinhead to explain the procedure to him. He explained about the courier checking names while the assistant shifted luggage from the counter to a trolley and out to the bus.

"And you saw this man do what?" the detective asked Sammy.

"Change Rat – Mountjoy's case. He'd already taken one load out and he came back and loaded up the trolley again. He'd put a few cases on, and he came to – to Mountjoy's, and he put that one on too, when he looked at it again, and suddenly bent and pulled up a case and swapped it with Mountjoy's."

"He pulled a case up from where?"

"Well," Sammy said, scratching his head, "I don't know exactly. Our duffelbags and stuff were just piled on the floor. I'd seen him fiddling with them before, while the names were being called out. I thought he was just checking to see they all had labels. He was doing *something* with labels, anyway. And he seemed to pull the case from there. Well! They'd had photos in all the papers of Ratbag's trumpet, so I thought maybe he was after it. So as soon as he turned away – and he had to go right up the counter for the next lot – I just swapped them over again. It seemed stupid when I'd done it, which is why I never – "

"Just a minute," the detective said. "He brought this other case with him – the one he swapped?"

"He must have."

"What kind of case?"

"The same as Mountjoy's."

"How did you know which was Mountjoy's?"

"Well, everyone knows that. It has this sign on it, a sort of rainbow."

"*Both* of them had rainbows?"

Sammy thought a moment. "They must have done. Only I had this feeling I was seeing double ... I was still trying to work out what happened when I was sick. Even *where* I was sick. It was like a dream ... "

Which was another thing I heard for the first time.

He said when he'd suddenly felt ill at the party he'd gone to find a bathroom. He'd tried a couple of rooms without success, but in one of them he'd surprised three or four men round a table. And he *had* surprised them. They'd all swung round as if they hadn't expected to be disturbed.

And what had given it the dreamlike feeling was that he knew one of the men but couldn't think how. He was so busy trying not to be sick that he shot right out of the room and tried another door and found a bathroom and was sick in the bowl right away. He felt so ill he had to stay there a few minutes. Then he washed his face and came back in the main room.

"And I still couldn't figure it out," he said. "I couldn't think how it was *possible* for me to know the man."

"The one you saw in the room?"

"Yes. And I've been thinking of it all day, trying to

put it together. Which I only did just as I was going off to sleep. Tonight. Is it still tonight?" he said, looking round.

Poor Sammy, he'd had a mixed-up time.

"Well. I did, anyway. He was in the travel agent's. I'd seen him a couple of days before – again only for a few seconds. But I definitely saw him, and he saw me." And he explained about our travel plans, how some of the kids hadn't managed to get the money together in time, how he'd gone up with one of them to the agent's the day before we left.

And here Skinhead cut in to explain about the agency itself. He said we'd used another one for previous school trips, but because so many were going this time he'd shopped around for a better deal; and in an educational paper had found this one advertising that they could beat anyone else on price. Their boss had come down to the school and promised us a beautiful deal – full courier service, with a tour of the city thrown in, and still cheaper than anyone else.

"Which it was," Skinhead said. "No complaints at all. They were very efficient, and the mix-up in arrangements certainly wasn't their fault."

"About your visit there," the inspector said, and turned to Sammy again. "What happened when you got to the agency?"

"Well, there was a bit of an argument. They said it was too late to take this kid. And I said it wasn't his fault, and we'd squeeze him in somehow, and anyway here was the money. So the clerk said he'd see what could be done, and went in an office next door. And I thought he

78

was trying to put me off, so I went in behind him. And we broke into a discussion there. The boss of the agency was having a row with a Chinese bloke. And this guy didn't want to be *seen*. He turned right round in his chair. He even got up and faced the other way! And the boss immediately got in a flap and said yes, yes, take the money, it'll be all right, and we went out of the room again. But that was the one. And that's where I'd seen him!"

"The Chinese man?"

"I think he was. That kind of face, anyway. So when I saw him again, in that room in Amsterdam, I thought I was dreaming. He did exactly the same thing! Just stared at me for a second or two, and turned round in his chair. But he definitely recognized me – I could see it. And then, I don't know how long after, but not long anyway, we got thrown out of the place."

"How did that happen?"

I told him how a man had suddenly come up and spoken to the owner of the place. How he'd changed from being a cheerful, amiable sort of person into practically a raving lunatic and told us all to beat it.

"Did *you* see this man who came and spoke to him – to recognize?" the inspector asked Sammy.

"Not to recognize. Not him. But that's what I was going to tell you. I recognized another one, next day. I mean, today. Is it?" he said helplessly. "I don't know where I am. But anyway the chap who turned up for the luggage – the assistant. He was in that room, too. Only when I saw him I thought I was seeing double again. I couldn't remember *where* I'd seen him. I was feeling so peculiar, you see. I'm sorry it's so complicated," Sammy said.

It *was* complicated, but everything was going very fast anyway. By this time the stuff we'd found in the case was being analysed. The chemistry annex of the university was next door to the police station, and by chance the CID's own scientist was working there late. He phoned just at that moment and the inspector took the call himself.

We saw him whistle a bit, and heard the scientist talking at the other end.

"Fine, hold it there. We'll get it ... Well," he said, putting the phone down. He seemed to shake himself a bit. "Eight hundred grams – over a pound and a half – of 98 per cent pure heroin. Once it's diluted that's worth about a hundred and fifty thousand pounds."

Ratbag had been very silent all this time, and the inspector nodded at him. "Quite a bag you had there, Ratbag."

What they worked out was this.

The travel agency offering such good deals was evidently in the drug-running business. By concentrating on schools they'd opened up an almost foolproof method. Teachers would accompany the school parties and take responsibility for the luggage. And a thoughtfully-provided courier service would ensure that everything went smoothly. Nobody had to hump his own bags: bag-humping service provided. Nobody had to open things for Customs inspection: Customs clearance also provided, with everything listed on one convenient form, signed for by the teacher in charge.

All they had to do, the inspector thought, was to identify one particular piece of luggage and copy it. This would be held ready for the return journey, just before the luggage went in, when the copied piece, containing drugs, would be switched with the original. The case of drugs would then go into the locked compartment and travel safely through Holland, Belgium and France to the hovercraft. It would cross the Channel to Dover where, with all the rest of the stuff it would simply be signed out by a Customs official and the teacher in charge, and be on its way.

At an already-established motorway stop everybody would get out for "rest room activities". The courier would distract the drivers while another employee, following behind with the original case, would open the compartment (duplicate key) and re-switch the cases. Foolproof. Except, on this occasion, it had gone wrong.

"You mean," Skinhead said, "because this boy already *had* re-switched the cases?"

"That's what he's told us."

"So the man was carrying – "

"The one with the drugs. Without knowing it. He probably crossed on that same hovercraft. It was very crowded, was it?"

"Packed," Skinhead said. "It was a job getting all the boys aboard."

"Exactly. Summer crossings ... You wouldn't have noticed him. He probably had the case in some kind of holdall. Just walked through with it, knowing he was safe – thinking so, anyway. And he got away with it.

Followed the bus by car. Did his little job, and in such a hurry that he wouldn't notice the difference in weight – only a pound and a half, after all. And was on his way. And will now be wondering", the inspector added, "where *his* case is. And how to get it."

In the pause Skinhead said hesitantly, "You don't think anyone is in any – danger?"

"With a hundred and fifty thousand pounds missing?"

"Well ... "

"The agency has the boys' addresses, does it?"

"Oh yes," Skinhead said. "Yes. They were very particular about that. In case any of the luggage got ... Oh."

"Yes," the inspector said.

Things started moving then.

Ten

Ratbag and his old lady weren't home that night. They went to stay with the friend they'd stayed with before. They told their landlady about it, and she told the reporter who rang up wanting to set up an interview with Ratbag for the following day.

The "reporter" rang up late, about eleven o'clock, and the police monitored the call. They were watching from a plumber's van, quietly parked in the street, when the break-in took place at two in the morning. They didn't interfere with the job. It was an efficient one with no glass broken and hardly anything at all to show, except for a bit of chipped woodwork near the catch on Ratbag's window.

When he came back next day Ratbag found the trumpet where he'd left it, in its case on the bed. The whole thing was a pound and a half lighter, and the trumpet sounded fine.

There'd been a discussion about whether to replace the heroin or substitute something else; and in the end the heroin had won. The argument was that it would certainly be tested right away, and if it was found to be worthless powder the distribution would be held up.

The police didn't want it held up. They wanted to watch what happened to it.

So it had gone back, everything, exactly as it was: the heroin, the packing, the velvet lining, the case.

And it had been followed, step by step.

And inside a week they had everything they needed: every detail of the agency, of the drug "holders", the peddlers, the users.

They could have gone ahead right then and smashed it. Which they were actually on the point of doing, when this guy turned up from Holland. He was a very nice guy, Groot. He was Inspector Groot. This very nice guy had a very crazy idea.

He turned up at the weekend, with a packet of photos and a video film. The three of us – Ratbag, Sammy, myself – went to the police station and looked at them. The photos were of various people and buildings, and the video was also of buildings – canalside mansions taken by day and by night.

We couldn't recognize the people in the photos, though one point was cleared up. Sammy's "Chinese" was probably East Indian. He paused longer over types from the East Indies, which seemed to please Groot. He said the East Indies were former Dutch colonies and many East Indians lived in Holland; several were on file in his own records, which gave him a better idea of the connection.

We didn't get far with the buildings, either. He tried to get us to remember what kind of gable the house had, and showed us enlargements of the three main kinds, the "bell" type, the "step" and the "neck". Sammy knew them already, and I remembered he was the only one to stay awake while the guide had droned on during our canal tour. He thought the house had a neck gable, a sort of curving top like an hourglass, but he'd only had a quick glance at it as we were driving away. He couldn't remember anything of the journey there.

The inspector noted this, and tried him for further details: whether the house had a date carved on it or any other decoration. But he couldn't remember. So Groot took us on another tack, "steering" us back along the route from the house to the hostel. But again it was inconclusive. All I remembered was rushing down narrow streets with water on all sides, and dozens of little bridges. And again it was Sammy who recalled something else.

He said, "I think there was a flower market – that floating one again."

"In which direction?"

Sammy closed his eyes. "Left, I think."

"You passed beside it?"

"Not really. It was just – away to the left."

"Was there a street name?"

Sammy thought, eyes still closed.

"I think Singer. We passed Singer again."

"Singer?" Groot was puzzled. "Perhaps Sin-*gel* ?"

"Perhaps."

"That was earlier," I said. "With Prince's Craft. When we went too far in the tram."

"Prince's Craft?" Groot was puzzled again. "Maybe – Prinsengracht?"

"It could be."

"You passed Prinsengracht also?"

"No, not then," Sammy said. "I don't remember it."

"One moment," Groot said, and studied a map, and became interested.

He tried hard with Prinsengracht, but couldn't budge Sammy. He just didn't remember it; which interested Groot all the more. He'd come to the conclusion that Sammy had been the most alert of the three of us, at least on the way back. He'd recalled a neck gable, and the flower market, and Singel. If he couldn't recall Prinsengracht, it was probably because we'd either passed it, or had actually been in it.

"Please try just a little harder," he said, and traced his finger on the map, showing us bridges and squares and monuments. But it was no good.

I thought my own description of the plushy place and of the attic might help, but it didn't. All the old mansions had attics, and many had preservation orders on them which meant they had to be kept as they were with all the old equipment intact. And because the mansions cost a fortune, only rich people lived in them, and they were all plushy. I couldn't remember details of the pictures, or the layout, or the furniture.

Even the names I dredged up – Nellie and Saskia, and Max and Danny and the rest – didn't get us anywhere, though he noted them down. They were common names, he said; quite common at the university. And there were ten thousand students at the university, many of the richer ones with little open cars. If we could remember what *kind* of car ... but we couldn't.

We stood there like lemons. We'd been somewhere and didn't know where. We couldn't remember how we'd gone there, or how we'd come back.

"All the same," Groot said, "I think there's something. I have to think about it a little."

Which he did.

As a consignment of heroin, 800 grams wasn't much; which was the worrying part. Small consignments, skillfully routed to one of many small dealers, were a bigger problem than single huge ones. When the police stepped on a big consignment they cut out, certainly, an important part of the trade. But an organization that could handle many *small* accounts was in every way more dangerous.

That's what Groot told them.

He said they could shut down this bit of it if they wanted. He couldn't stop them. They'd be congratulated. He just pleaded with them not to. It was the *big* people he was after, the suppliers, the organization.

He said Amsterdam was becoming the chief supply center for the west: it was because of its nearness to Rotterdam, now the most important seaport in the world. As the detection rate for air smuggling improved, the traders were turning to ships. Aircraft were easy to check, but not ships; and particularly not ships in the overcrowded port of Rotterdam.

For two years now he'd been working on a connection between Holland and the former colonies in the East Indies. The heroin didn't come from there: it came from Pakistan and Burma. But shipping lines from the

East Indies operated everywhere, with a steady stream of cargo coming into the Europort of Rotterdam. The profits of drug smuggling were so enormous that the costs of routing the stuff right round the world weren't important. What was important was control of the transport, and of the business side. And all Rotterdam's business was run from Amsterdam.

He said his department had a team of accountants checking literally hundreds of thousands of transactions – of private banks, shipping lines, trading firms – all connected in some way with the east. They were looking for a loophole; for something that couldn't quite be explained, either in the movement of money, or of goods, or of people.

Now, Groot said, it looked as if something had turned up. And with a very small transaction, which was exciting. They'd always known their best chance of success would be with a small deal rather than a big one. Less attention would be paid to detail, more chance of someone making a mistake, of an accident happening.

And a mistake had been made here. An accident had happened here! A boy had seen someone, and then something, that he wasn't supposed to see.

He thought it had happened like this.

The travel agency had been chosen to shift a consignment. The boss of this agency had picked a particular school for the job, perhaps from among several others. Because the consignment was small, it needed only a small container; and a musical instrument case was ideal for the purpose. The courier would have had the task of selecting a particular case for switching – with Ratbag's,

88

so easily identifiable, practically selecting itself. This would have been noted on the outward journey, so that a duplicate could be arranged for the return one.

The difficulty which had led Sammy to visit the agency and spot the man in the back room, was the first slip-up. But still nothing might have come of it without the second. And this was the incredible stroke of luck they'd been waiting for. To see a man in a back room in England (even a man who obviously didn't want to be seen) was one thing. To see the same man again in a back room in Amsterdam was quite another. And for an alert and imaginative schoolboy – Groot talking – it was enough!

But still there'd been more ... For in the room there had also been the individual selected to make the switch for the return journey. And here was the inexcusable error, said Groot. Here was the careless mistake that he'd known would one day open up the case. For they had gone right ahead using the same man!

Everything had followed from this: the boy had recognized the baggage handler in the morning, had seen him fiddle with the labels and switch the case. Had then himself switched it back again. And by chance had found himself in position with a pair of binoculars when the incident took place on the motorway in England.

"Yes, yes, I know," Groot said. "It is all, for us, incredible luck. But aren't we owed some luck after two years? Always I've known something like this would happen. Please don't spoil it all now. Please let me and my colleagues ride with the luck – for just a few weeks. In fact, for three weeks. For three weeks exactly!"

Why three weeks exactly?

He'd dreamed up his plan.

In three weeks exactly Ratbag would be going back to Amsterdam. That was the date van Bergh had set for the audition.

We'd got nowhere with the photographs and the video; but still by patient questioning he had dragged some further and valuable details from us. From things we had said he was sure we would remember more. He didn't at this time wish to press us more and perhaps distort what was buried in our minds. But it was there, he was sure of it. And in Amsterdam it would come back.

The café we would find again. The students we would perhaps encounter again. Through them, or by ourselves, we might find the house again.

Already, from what we had said, he had an idea in which area the house must be. But he wouldn't influence us. He wouldn't jeopardize two years of work by any rash or hasty move. Also he wouldn't alert anyone by following up the details so far supplied. Nobody would be questioned, followed, investigated in any way. Nothing at all would happen until we had returned to Amsterdam, and safely left it again.

So who were "we"?

Ratbag and me. Sammy had already seen too much, and had been. So no Sammy. But Ratbag had to go in any case: this was already known. And it was entirely natural if he were accompanied by a friend.

There would be no danger, Groot said. He could guarantee that, 100 per cent.

That's what he said.

Eleven

So OK, there we were again. Amsterdam, August, the place still crowded, and I hated the sight of it.

I had a sick feeling that I shouldn't be here. I'd had it when I got up, and on the plane, and in the car from the airport. No student hostel for us this time. We'd been booked into the Grand Hotel Tivoli (courtesy of the van Bergh Trust) and given fifty quid to spend in Dutch money, and I still hated it. My stomach was turning over.

Two letters were waiting at the desk for Ratbag, and he opened them while I looked at the room (two king-size beds, amazing fancy furniture), and at the bathroom, and at the balcony outside. We were on the twelfth floor, and the view was stunning. You could see practically the whole town. I saw the mansion-lined canals, and the floating flower market and even, a bit to one side, the square with the little streets of jazz cafés. My stomach had calmed down a bit while I looked round the room, but it started up again then so I skipped the view and went back in.

Ratbag was frowning over one of the letters. The first was from van Bergh's secretary with a mention about when our return flight would be booked. Meanwhile a car would call for him at ten sharp in the morning, and he had to be waiting below. It was the other he was frowning at.

"Who's Wim?" he said.

"Wim?"

I looked at the letter. It was typed on plain paper.

Dear Paul,

　　Really glad you are back here. I wish you all success with your audition. Meanwhile enjoy your stay and I hope the view from the balcony recalls interesting memories. A friend will contact you.

　　　　　　　　　　　　　　　　Sincerely, Wim

"This has to be Groot," I said.

"Well, why doesn't he say so?" He looked at the letter again. "And whose friend, his or ours?"

"Nobody's," I said. "It'll be another copper."

He grunted and returned to the first letter, and shook his head. "Ten in the morning!" he said. "I don't play good in the morning. I need sleep tonight."

I hoped he'd get some, and plenty of it.

I hoped everybody would.

We rested a while, and went down about five for something to eat. The place had a big tea terrace outside under an awning. It was pretty crowded and we looked for an empty table.

"Hi Paul, Hi Nicky," somebody said. A young guy in jeans had spread himself all over a table. He was sprawled in one chair, had a leather jacket on another, and a parcel on a third. "Sit down. I'm Karl."

I wondered if this was Wim's "friend", but didn't ask in case he turned out to be somebody else's.

"Wim said to look out for you," he said, settling the question, and shifting stuff so we could sit, "so I kept a couple of places. I figured you'd be down. Say, what do you guys want – tea, coffee, cake, sandwiches?" He spoke like an American, but he wasn't one. Plenty seemed to be around, though, and he fitted in easily.

In no time he'd ordered the lot and was chatting away, giving us all the news. He knew about the room on the twelfth floor and said Wim had switched us to it himself "for your convenience". He also knew about the audition, and gave more information on it. Van Bergh had a concert in the evening, he said, and wanted to rehearse in the afternoon, which accounted for the morning call. Ratbag wasn't the only one he was auditioning. There were two other candidates, and if he couldn't decide which one to choose he'd ask them back for another audition the following day.

Ratbag's face dropped at the mention of other candidates, and so did mine; for a different reason. I'd been wondering why our return flights *hadn't* been booked. The letter from van Bergh's secretary had just said the matter would be attended to when plans were clarified. I saw what needed clarifying now: they didn't know if we'd be staying over another day.

This set me in a panic. I'd worked out something while resting up in the room. We didn't *have* to get in any funny situations. It was obvious Groot didn't know which café we'd visited, or the people we'd met, or the house we'd been in. It was why I was here – to see if I could remember. And I did remember now. I'd felt it while we were driving into town; had been certain of it when looking down from the balcony, and ever since. The whole flavor of the place had suddenly hit me again.

I could remember the street where the café was; even details about it I'd barely noticed at the time. There'd been a crooked post stuck in the road some distance before the café to stop traffic going farther. The car – this occurred to me while lying on the bed – must have mounted the pavement there before whizzing along it to stop outside. And the faces of the students as they'd come streaming into the glassed-in veranda. And the dizzy tangled-up drive to the house, and swaying about on the pavement outside when we got out.

There'd been a footbridge over the canal directly opposite and a couple of the students had larked about on it, pretending to dive in, while the front door was being opened. And the door itself: there'd been something distinctive about the light over it. The fitment was in the form of a sea creature, a dolphin or a serpent or a flying fish. I couldn't remember which, but I was pretty sure I would if I saw it again.

Not one detail of this had occurred to me at home, yet all of it had come drifting back now. And I'd planned what to do about it. Stay away from these places. At least make no kind of identification or show I remembered them in any way. I knew Ratbag couldn't. He hadn't remembered a single thing during our questioning. He'd been too involved with the music at the time, either listening to it, or playing and singing; also he'd drunk too much.

And what could they expect of us, anyway? If we'd be in town for only a few hours we couldn't go poking about everywhere. To drift around for an hour or two this evening was OK with me; then early to bed for Ratbag's audition tomorrow, and safely off home after it. *Then* I'd tell what I remembered. Then they could get on with it.

Except it didn't look that way now. Not if we had to stay here two days. And two nights. With Ratbag very noticeable during all the drifting about we might have to do ...

Karl noticed our expressions, and came to the wrong conclusion. "Hey, if you guys are worried at running short of money over an extra day," he said, "don't be. You run short, you tell someone."

"Tell who?" I said.

"You're under surveillance the whole time. Right this minute we're being watched. Everywhere you go, every step you take, someone is there. If you want to make a contact, here's what you do."

He told us what to do. We had to drop a book; in fact to be on the safe side, to drop it twice. He had the book there with him. It was in the parcel he'd had on the chair; now on the table and covered with crumbs. It was a guide of Amsterdam, with a big fold-up map stuck in it. What we had to do was open the book, and while spreading the map to fumble and drop it. Twice. Then make for the nearest café or street bench, where someone would join us and help "study the map".

"You guys got that?"

"Yeah," I said, and hoped we wouldn't be using the terrific idea.

"So here's the next thing. Don't open it now, but you'll find a few routes marked on the map. Wim wants you to take a stroll tonight. Try the Leidseplein first, see if you meet any old friends in a certain place. If so, great. You say you want to be pen pals, exchange names, addresses. If not, too bad tonight ... So you take the other strolls, you'll see where. And remember, every second someone is with you, OK?"

I said OK and in about a minute he was gone, leaving us the parcel; also the bill for tea.

Ratbag and I looked at each other.

"Another audition!" he said blankly.

"There might not be," I said.

But I had a funny feeling that there might.

Twelve

We took the book out for a walk that night. We had a snack in the hotel first, and Ratbag just signed the bill for it. He'd done the same at tea, for we'd found out van Bergh would be picking up the tab for everything in the hotel; the best news we'd had so far.

It was a warm night, very humid, and the floodlighting had come on everywhere. The crowded square was easily visible even at street level, so we didn't bother with a tram and just walked there. Ratbag was very silent, still brooding over his audition, which was fine with me. I didn't want him brooding over cafés.

I'd worked out what to do now. We'd make a tour of the main café streets, and I'd pick a couple of wrong ones; then we'd do the other tour, where I'd also "see nothing". By which time I could remind him of tomorrow's audition, and that would be it. End night patrol.

The second tour was bugging me worse than the first. For one thing, the map supplied by Groot turned out to have a large stamp impressed on it saying it was police property: not a promising start for a confidential job. It was probably an office slip-up, but there could be others. I was scared even to be carrying it.

Also, I'd seen that the tours he'd marked in had been shrewdly chosen. Evidently relying on Sammy's floating flower market being "away to the left", he'd placed the tours to the right of it, and cunningly spread them. One was certainly the route the girl had taken to drive us back – and I could practically visualize it now.

Worse still, I'd pinpointed the bridge where I'd seen the students pretending to dive in. I'd even recalled something else about it. I remembered I'd seen them only because Ratbag had swung me round to look. He'd been pretty blotto at the time, laughing his head off and pointing. I was surprised to remember it at all, and only hoped he wouldn't.

First things first, though. Cafés.

There seemed to be a different crowd in town now: older people, fewer students. The square was jam-packed with them when we got to it, and we threaded our way slowly across. Various "turns" were performing: jugglers, mime-shows, guitarists, even a guy playing the bagpipes. We edged through and entered the back streets, and right off I saw the real one and began sweating. The crooked post was stuck in the middle of the street not more than fifty yards up it. I hadn't realized it was so close. I could see the café itself, outlined with light bulbs, and the glassed-in veranda.

I prayed Ratbag wouldn't notice, and he didn't, and straight away I steered him past it to the next street, and we began inspecting cafés there. He sharpened up a bit then. Jazz was thumping out on all sides, and several of the places had glassed-in verandas: it was the general style of the area, which was another thing I'd forgotten.

98

He paused uncertainly at one, so I stared hard at it too.

"What do you think?" he said.

"We could see."

We went in, and I spotted immediately it was nothing like the other place. Unfortunately he spotted it too, so we went out and carried on up the street.

This happened a couple of times more before we got lost in the maze and started working our way back. And by this time I was sweating hard, for he was getting the feel of the place now and remembering more.

"Hang on," he said, "wasn't it round here Sammy was checking the menus?"

"He was checking menus everywhere."

"No, here ... I've been here before," he said suddenly. Which was right: he had. Somehow we'd got back to the right street again, from the other end. It was narrow and twisty here, but I could see the top of the crooked post, two or three hundred yards away.

"Let's stop for a drink, then," I said. *And waste some time.*

"In a minute." He was high-footing it ahead, looking from side to side. "Somewhere here," he said. "I'm sure of it. And real near.".Which it was: we were practically there. Then we *were* there, and he slowly passed it, and stopped and came back, and my toes began to curl.

"It's this one," he said.

"Is it?"

He looked at me, then back at the place, and walked in, and I followed him. A waiter bustled up, balancing four drinks and four plates of cake, and said, "No room", and then had a double-take and said, "Hello! The trumpeter!" and I felt my heart tumble on the floor and go rolling away somewhere.

In no time he'd dumped his load and was shaking us both by the hand and saying hang on, he'd find us a place. And in a few seconds he had, steering us through the packed veranda and inside to a table in a dark corner, and apologizing for it, and shifting people along.

"Wonderful to see you back," he said. "Ach, that night! You played like an angel."

"Well, thanks," Ratbag said, his face splitting in a grin. "Any of the old gang here, then?"

"Old gang?"

"The students we were here with."

"Ah, students. Not students. After the festival students take jobs, make money," the old guy said, smiling. "Maybe one or two come later. You play for us again tonight?"

"He can't tonight, we're only staying a few minutes," I said quickly, and I said it with relief. I'd seen it wasn't only the students who weren't here but the original band wasn't either. Different band, different customers: the whole population seemed to have changed, as in the square. They were an older crowd now, mainly tourists.

"So what can I get you?"

We had a couple of Cokes, and he wouldn't take the money, so we left with our fifty quid still intact.

"You know it's a funny thing," Ratbag said. He'd grown very cheerful since the waiter said he was an angel. "When you got no money you really need it, and when you got it they won't take it."

"Yeah, life's strange."

"But we found the right café," he said, looking at me. "What you so miserable about?"

I wasn't miserable. I just saw he'd sharpened up too much round here. He'd remembered what I hadn't expected him to, and I didn't want it to become a habit.

We hit the main canals about nine o'clock, and I was stiff with nervous exhaustion. Nervous something, anyway. I'd dreamed up a new idea and it tired me so much I could hardly walk straight. I knew he'd recognized the café only after he'd got the feel of the place and had something to compare it with. I was going to take him past the house right off, cold, before he knew where he was. The idea frightened me so much I had to force myself into the Prinsengracht before I changed my mind.

He didn't notice the street sign. It was right there on the corner, and screaming away, but he didn't notice: too busy talking. He'd suddenly become very chatty, which was OK with me. Anything that took his mind off the surroundings was OK. But his rusty voice, yodelling away, was giving me a headache.

It was very quiet along this bit of the canal; a high-class part of town. We'd left the crowds behind and the only sounds were the distant clang of a tram or the hoot of a car. Every few minutes a canal boat glided softly past, the long line of port-holes showing candle-lit diners and waiters pouring wine. Apart from the odd couples snogging on shadowy benches it was about the only movement.

I wondered if we *were* being kept under surveillance and turned for a quick look.

"What is it?" Ratbag said.

"I wondered how far we'd come."

But I'd spotted him: a distant figure, cigar glowing in mouth, innocently strolling behind us. It wasn't all I spotted. We'd walked far enough now to get a perspective, and I'd recognized it; recognized it without a doubt. The curve of the canal, the pattern of the buildings, the floating flower market "away to the left"; all as when we'd jetted along it with the girl that night. This was the street all right, and my stomach turned over again.

"They really got style here," Ratbag was saying. "I mean, the way the leaves are glowing in the trees, and the buildings and everything. You got to admire it."

"Yeah," I said, and admired it, and only wished I was a million miles away. The leaves *were* glowing, a brilliant emerald green, totally unreal in the concealed lighting overhead. And the houses just as unreal; a stately row of them, brilliant as spotlit exhibits in a museum, their reflections quivering in the water.

"And the bridges – the way they got them outlined with little lights. It's like, you know, like fairyland," Ratbag said.

"Yeah."

I didn't want him watching bridges. I was counting bridges. We'd passed two, and there was one to go before *the* bridge, the one opposite the house. I could see it already. I could even see the house. I kept woodenly on. Take him past it. Give no sign: to him, or to the glowing cigar behind. And when we were well beyond, point out the time and cross the canal and take him back another way.

We came to the next bridge and passed it, and approached the dangerous one, Ratbag still cackling away. He was on to food now, and how he liked it here, and the liveliness of the town, and the friendliness of the waiter. I didn't even answer him now, my mouth too dry. We were at the bridge. And no question about it! It was smaller than the others, a lower balustrade; maybe why the students had pretended to dive from it. And were level with the house itself, and something had begun happening to my hair. It was rising at the back.

With the strangest floating feeling I went past it, only wishing Ratbag would dry up now. His crazy cracked voice seemed to bounce back off the walls. I was petrified someone would come out and spot him. But nobody did. The house stood silent as the grave, unlit inside, brilliantly floodlit outside, with the fixture switched on over the door. Just as I'd remembered: a marine creature. A flying fish. I couldn't see the number. But I'd seen enough.

I let another bridge pass, weak with relief, and looked at my watch and said, "Here, Ratbag – ten o'clock! You haven't forgotten the audition in the morning?"

"Hey!" he said, and his face fell. "I did."

So, exactly as planned, the talk session ended, and also the walk session. We crossed the canal, cut back by another route, and by ten thirty were in the hotel.

He undressed silently and got into bed, and after a minute I put the light out and said goodnight.

He didn't answer, and I blinked a bit in the dark and thought over the evening. The café found, and the house found. If we could get off on the afternoon plane, that was it.

I heard him turn over and sigh a bit in the dark, and half of me was sorry at deceiving him tonight, but half of me wasn't.

Thirteen

He was gargling when I woke and I looked at my watch and saw it wasn't seven o'clock yet. I got up and went in the bathroom and found him pulling faces in the mirror. He'd washed and dressed already and was doing some kind of lip exercises.

"It's a bit early," I said.

"I got to loosen up."

He carried on pulling faces, so I took a shower and dressed. He was very nervous. He couldn't keep still. He went out to the balcony and came back in. He put his trumpet together and tooted a bit, then cursed and went back in the bathroom and pulled faces again.

I went out to the balcony myself. It was going to be a hot day. There was a mist over the town and it had a tired used-up look. I felt the same way myself. I figured we'd walked four or five miles yesterday, apart from the flight. I seemed to be aching all over.

We went down to breakfast at eight, and he ate practically nothing. Then we went back to the room and he tried to play again, and cursed again.

"Relax," I told him.

"I got to practice. I can't here."

We went out to the garden at the back and he practised

there; except the gardeners came and watched, which put him off, so we took a walk to a small park, and he tried again.

That was no use either, and his face was twitching and sweating.

"I told you – I can't do it in the morning. I got to loosen up," he said despairingly.

"Well, take a jog."

"OK."

I sat on a bench with his trumpet while he took one. He went fast round the park three times, and was starting a fourth when I stopped him. "OK, you've done enough." He was sweating like a horse, but he wasn't twitching any more. Also, it was past nine o'clock, and the car was due at ten.

We went back to the hotel and he showered off, and went prowling round the room in a towel, snapping his fingers and jiggling his shoulders. But he was looser now, and picking up his feet in the old crazy way again.

We went down a few minutes before time, and the car came sharp on the hour. It was a big Mercedes, and we piled in the back and drove to the Concertgebouw.

"You come in with me, OK?" he said.

"Well, if they let me."

"Come in. I know you *got* to be there," he said.

He had that strange look on his face again, so I didn't argue with him.

Someone was waiting at the door, and as we followed through the foyer and down corridors I saw big photos of van Bergh everywhere. We went to a small suite of rooms at the back. Van Bergh's secretary was in one, and she went through to another and presently popped her head out and beckoned to Ratbag.

He clutched at my sleeve, and we went forward together.

"Just Mr Mountjoy," the woman said.

"And him. He's coming with me," Ratbag said, and pushed past and I tagged along, embarrassed.

Van Bergh was sitting at a table looking at a pile of music, and he looked up at the disturbance in the doorway. The secretary said something to him in Dutch, and he got up and came towards us.

"Paul Mountjoy," he said, and shook Ratbag's hand, smiling, then glanced at me.

"He's come with me," Ratbag said huskily, "if that's OK with – "

"It's all right," van Bergh said, and dismissed his secretary. He didn't shake hands with me, but flapped his hand for me to sit in a corner, and took Ratbag's arm and led him to a chair by the table. "I hear nice things of you, Paul," he said, his eyes crinkling. He was older than in his photos, but a handsome old guy; big flexible mouth, big face altogether, bushy eyebrows. "You played the Dirksen concerto in England, right?"

"Yeah, right," Ratbag said.

"Whose idea was that – yours or the music teacher's?"

"Well, I – I didn't do the programing," Ratbag stammered.

"It's a joke," van Bergh said, and chuckled to show what a big one it was. "That concerto was dedicated to me, so it was *good* programing. But you played well, very well. What do you want to play me now?"

Ratbag fiddled in his case and got out his music. Skinhead had given him duplicate scores, so van Bergh could check him.

The old man glanced at them, and turned and fished around on some shelves behind him. He had a stack of records there, and he picked one out and put it on a record player. The room filled with music from a pair of big speakers, and he hunted a little for the track he wanted. "The second movement, right? Twelve, fifteen bars before the solo. Fix your instrument and we'll hear a little meanwhile."

Ratbag put the trumpet together, rather shakily, and stretched his mouth a bit while the music continued.

"Your mouth – not so good in the morning, eh?" the old man said.

"Yeah, right!" Ratbag said, sweating.

"The same with me. It's why I rehearse in the afternoon. Say when you're ready."

"I'm ready," Ratbag said.

Van Bergh took the arm off the record.

"I'll play it again softly," he said, "so you have orchestral time. Keep to time but don't copy the solo."

"That's you on solo," Ratbag said.

"You recognize my faults?"

"You did good," Ratbag said.

What staggered me was the way he was talking to him. He was nervous, but only about the test. He wasn't nervous of van Bergh. Yet this was a world-famous musician. The huge concert hall was papered with his portraits. And the sign out front said his concert was totally sold out.

Van Bergh just raised his eyebrows, didn't say anything. Then he put the arm back on the record and nodded to Ratbag and sat down. And Ratbag stood up. He didn't bother with the sheet music, just closed his eyes and waited till the trumpet came in on the record, and came in himself.

For a moment or two I couldn't tell any difference. Then he got it wrong somewhere and the timing went out. He just nodded, with closed eyes, and missed a few notes and slurred a few, and came in again strongly. But now the difference was there you couldn't mistake it. The trumpet on the record was smooth and flexible, and his own sounded rasping and awkward. I knew he'd practised endlessly; had heard him a few times, and each time had sounded great to me. And this time was really no different, despite his early-morning stiffness. The difference was hearing him play note for note with a world master; and it was enormous – a thing I hadn't been able to appreciate before.

The movement ended, and van Bergh took the record off and selected another, without speaking. And the same thing took place. He played a section to let Ratbag hear the timing, then went back and let him play it in concert. They did three short pieces this way, and in between Ratbag looked at me. I couldn't read his expression. I couldn't read van Bergh's, either. Then it had ended, and van Bergh switched the record player off.

"You play jazz, I believe," he said.

"Some."

"Play."

Ratbag didn't ask what he wanted, just closed his

eyes and tooted a bit, then stretched his mouth and went into "Basin Street". He played it straight, fairly brassy, a way I'd heard him play it before, and then seemed to finish, and van Bergh said, "Good", and picked up a pen and began writing.

But Ratbag hadn't finished. He hadn't sat down or even opened his eyes. He was swaying slightly, and he suddenly picked up where he'd left off and seemed to turn the music inside out. He went rippling up and down the scales, tying the tune in knots and untying it in a brilliant series of variations. And I saw van Bergh sitting back in his chair and staring at him. Then Ratbag held one note, held it like a sort of cry – for three seconds, and four and five, as if at the last gasp in Basin Street. Except it wasn't.

Stunned out of my head, I realized it was the first note of the classical concerto he'd played right at the very beginning; and he began playing it through again; played about a whole minute of it, very calmly and serenely. But it wasn't classical now, and it wasn't jazz either. There was a kind of humorous mocking tone that I'd heard from him before – the very first time he'd played for Skinhead.

He put the trumpet down and smiled a bit crookedly.

Van Bergh was still staring at him.

"Why did you do that?" he said.

"You said not to copy the solo."

Van Bergh stared longer, then resumed his writing.

"What makes you so angry?" the old man said.

"I'm not angry."

Van Bergh finished writing, then stared some more.

"Paul, I'll tell you," he said. "You have great talent, but whether for jazz trumpet or classical I can't say."

"The concerto was no good, eh?"

"I didn't say that. It lacked polish, but there was great ability. You covered your mistakes, kept the feeling, slurred skillfully. I was impressed. But perhaps the classical discipline hampers your freshness, your spontaneity?"

"I know I got a lot to learn," Ratbag mumbled.

"True. And you will. I note you have absolute pitch, incidentally ... However, there are problems."

He rubbed his face for a while.

"If I give you a scholarship you must come to New York for at least a month a year. I hold master classes there during my winter season. And the same for a month a year in Amsterdam. And you are the youngest pupil I have ever considered. Many problems ... For instance, education, accommodation. The Trust could cope with them, at no expense to you, but then there are further ones, professional ones. I would wish you to have orchestral experience, to make recordings."

"A professional orchestra? Recordings?" Ratbag said. He was still standing, but his knees seemed to wobble and he sat down then.

"Certainly. Which in view of your age would raise some issues with the musicians' unions, management. As well as requiring from you a complete dedication to *classical* music. You see?"

"Yeah," Ratbag said.

"Don't be disheartened. In fact I can tell you", van Bergh said slowly, "that in a normal year I would have no hesitation in awarding you a scholarship right away."

"You mean that?" Ratbag said.

"For sure," van Bergh said seriously. "However, it isn't a normal year. Pack up your trumpet now ... It happens there are two other candidates, of the highest merit – one already a young professional musician, the other in his final year at college. With neither of whom the same problems arise. So I can't say yet. I will hear them both this morning. Perhaps I will hear all of you again tomorrow. What I want you to do", he said, rising, "is to be at your hotel at one o'clock, and my secretary will call you there to let you know. *If* I hear you again, it will be in a different order."

We'd both stood up with him, and he opened a drawer and took an envelope out.

"Meanwhile," he said, "two tickets for my concert tonight ... They'll fetch a lot of money out there if you want to sell them."

"Jeeze, no. Thanks," Ratbag said. "I mean, thanks a lot, Mr van Bergh. I mean, for everything."

"My pleasure. And my privilege," van Bergh said, and shook hands with him, and nodded at me, and we were out.

Fourteen

In the street Ratbag was still dazed. "New York, Amsterdam," he muttered. "I couldn't do that. How could I do it?"

"Why couldn't you?" I said.

"My old lady – who'd look after her? I couldn't do it."

"Well, he hasn't offered you it yet."

"Yeah, right. Let's sit down somewhere. I need a drink."

I needed one, too. Apart from the general excitement, it had turned very hot. The mist had lifted and the sun was scorching down. The streets were full of slow-moving tourists, taking photos of each other. We found a café and sat outside.

"Mijnheer?" a waiter said.

"Coke, please," I said.

"Beer," Ratbag said. "Three."

The waiter looked at him. "Three beers?"

"Yeah."

"Three beers, one Coke," the waiter said and went off, and I stared at Ratbag.

"Boy, I need it," he said. "That was quite a session. How you think I did in there?"

"He liked you. He said so."

"That's a smart old guy," he said thoughtfully. "He saw I was feeling ... Well, he knew how I'm feeling."

I wasn't too clear myself, but he still seemed edgy so I kept quiet. A blind man with a stick was tapping his way along the tables and I watched him. He came to ours and paused and I thought for a moment he was begging, but he was only feeling the chairs.

"The place is free?" he said in English.

"Sure."

He lowered himself to a seat and slightly raised his panama hat to mop his brow. "So how are you boys doing today?" he said, and peered over his dark glasses and I saw it was Groot.

The waiter came up with the drinks at that moment and set them on the table, so I didn't say anything. "Mijnheer?" he said to Groot. And Groot felt a bit blindly with his hand and touched the frosted beer cans and said he'd have one himself. And apart from commenting on the weather he said nothing more till the waiter had brought it.

"How did the audition go?" he said.

"I got to go back tomorrow."

"As I thought ... It's not good to drink much beer on a hot day," he said mildly. Ratbag had drained one can and was opening another. "There are still things for you to do. You found the café last night, I understand."

"Yeah, but not the students."

"Not at that time. Some came later – two did. Members of my staff waited there. But as I promised we're not checking anything yet ... You didn't manage to find the house, then?"

His dark glasses were turned towards me, and I looked at Ratbag.

"Not that we spotted," he said.

"You walked a long way down the Prinsengracht." Groot had poured his beer in a glass and was sipping it, his dark glasses still on me.

"The houses look alike", I said, "to a stranger."

"Quite. But you noticed *nothing* familiar, nothing at all?"

I looked at Ratbag again. He'd practically finished another can, and he wiped his mouth.

"Well, yeah," he said, "we did. It was all familiar, wasn't it?"

"All of it," I said thankfully.

Groot drank a little more beer. He didn't say anything for a while, but he didn't take his eyes off me either.

"The waiter told the young people", he said, "that you were back in town, which they were glad to hear. They will be looking out for you – I am sure at the café. I would like you to go there again tonight."

"We can't tonight," Ratbag said. "We're going to a concert. Mr van Bergh gave us tickets."

Groot thought about it.

"It's not a difficulty," he said. "The concert should end by nine. You can easily be at the café by half past. That's when the students came last night."

"See, I don't want a late night," Ratbag told him. "I maybe got an early audition in the morning."

"How early?"

"I'll know when we get back to the hotel. They're

calling me at one o'clock."

"So I'll call you soon after ... Paul, I truly want your success," Groot said seriously. He stared at him a few moments. "Believe me, I mean it. But this other matter is of – such importance. So many lives being ruined. You'll know what I mean, perhaps." He fumbled in his pocket and brought out some coins and put them on the table. "Please help me with it. I'll hope for a late audition."

He didn't look at me again, just got up and tapped off with his stick, and Ratbag stared after him.

"Well, that's right," he said, "about lives being ruined. It's really right! I've seen it."

He was brooding, and I suddenly realized I hadn't been so clever. I could have told Groot right then about the house. It wouldn't have been easy, after keeping quiet to Ratbag about it. Not easy, but not impossible. I hadn't *denied* seeing it, after all. I just hadn't mentioned it. I might have claimed I didn't want to worry him before his audition. I might have, but I hadn't. And now I couldn't. The best thing, I thought, would be if they canned the audition altogether. Then we could go off this afternoon and that would finish it. They could can it either because van Bergh was giving him the scholarship, or because he wasn't. And I didn't care which.

This thought made me feel so lousy, I drained my Coke suddenly. My mouth was still dry, and he still had beer in the can, so I had a drink of that too. The beer was sour after the coke, as sour as I felt myself, and I thought boy, what a stinker I was turning into.

We were at the hotel when the call came at one. The auditions were on for tomorrow. Ratbag's was the last, at twelve. We could go to the café tonight. I didn't know whether to be sorry or glad about any of this. I didn't know how to be any more.

We took a walk in the afternoon, covering the other routes on the map. I felt sick at still stringing him along. He didn't say much, very broody. He hadn't said much when the call came. I'd tried to get him to talk.

"You still got a chance then, Ratbag," I'd told him.

"He's giving me it."

"I told you – he liked you."

"He's giving me the scholarship."

I stared at him. "Did he say that?"

"No. Only he took me first today to get me out the way. I knew that. Tomorrow he'll get the others out the way."

"You *know* it?"

"I've got it. It's mine. I don't want to talk about it."

I couldn't tell if it was the beer, or his whole un-balanced nature – totally uncertain one moment, totally confident the next. I didn't know what to make of him. But I never had.

A few drops of rain had fallen in the afternoon, and in the evening the air was heavy with thunder. We had a bite in the hotel and took off for the concert. Cars and taxis were milling about outside the hall, and a regiment of police seemed to be there. Apparently the Queen was expected, and a red carpet was out.

We felt like tramps going in. We just had our jeans on and denim jackets. Ratbag was even wearing his odd sneakers. The usher looked twice at us after seeing our tickets. We'd been given the best seats in the house – up front, center stage! The people on either side looked at us strangely, too. They were all in evening dress, the women in costly jewelry.

The whole house rose as the Queen entered the royal box, and there was a drum roll before the national anthem began. Then the audience settled and the concert started.

I don't know how it was. I was too worried about the rest of the evening to pay any attention. Van Bergh certainly got a colossal hand, and stood there pretty relaxed, his big floppy mouth smiling, bowing first to the royal box and then the audience.

Ratbag listened hard to him, but his mood was still strange, his eyes glittering. He seemed restless, hardly even interested in the rest of the concert. I caught him looking at his watch once; but he sat up again when van Bergh reappeared for the last item.

It was a special one, and the old man said a few words first in Dutch – apparently something funny, for the whole house broke up and began looking at the Queen, who was laughing and clapping. Then he raised his trumpet slightly to her, and began a series of lively tunes, the orchestra accompanying him, and everyone seemed to know them for the whole house began to clap and stamp in time.

They didn't want to let him go, and he had to play again and again, maybe for another twenty minutes.

Then he hung his head, pleading exhaustion, and in a final burst of cheering was allowed to leave the stage. And we were streaming out in a huge hubbub of talk and laughter.

People had become separated in the scrum and were calling to each other, and I heard someone yelling "Polly!" But I still didn't cotton on till people behind began nudging us, and I turned and saw her. The girl who'd jetted us along that night! She was hooting away in Dutch, waving to attract our attention, and two familiar faces were with her, and it was "Paulie!" she was yelling, and to Ratbag, and my heart gave a single massive thump and I wanted to drop through the floor.

In seconds she'd pushed her way through and was hugging us, and the others were doing the same.

"It's Nellie – remember? And here's Saskia and Max. Lovely to see you! We hoped we would. Come, we'll go back to my place – where we were before, just a little party, two or three others coming along later. The car's outside. Oh, I'm so glad we met!"

We were being swept along by the crowd, and I hoped against hope that we'd somehow lose them as we spilled out into the street. But as we hit the foyer a new situation had developed. The whole mob had bunched up there, struggling into raincoats, trying to open umbrellas. A colossal rainstorm was under way outside, the night alive with thunder and lightning. And Nellie was still hanging on to Ratbag, and Saskia to me. And somehow we'd become Paulie and Nicky now, and I remembered they'd been calling us that the first ghastly time we'd met.

Out in the street, rain was bouncing off the pavements,

people splashing about and yelling for taxis; and we stumbled all in a heap over to the car. It wasn't far away but we were wet through before we got to it. The whole interior of the car was swimming, the roof still down. They spent a couple of minutes getting it up, and I pulled Ratbag to one side and said in his ear, "Ratbag, we can't go with them! We can't!"

"Why not?"

"We're not supposed to go into the house!"

"But we'll find out where it is. They're taking us to it!"

"Ratbag, honest – "

"Have you forgotten why we're here? *I'm* going."

"Ratbag, listen. We *can't* go in there!"

I was yelling now, and Nellie heard and mistook me. "Sure you can – plenty of room. Paulie, with me in the front. Nicky in the back with Max and Saskia. Come on, dive in!"

And he was in, and so was I, in a sopping mess in the back with the other two. And as we took off, one last feverish thought. I was still hanging on to the guidebook. In this crazy disordered shambles, could the guys following possibly be hanging on to us?

And the journey back – the route I knew so well now, but slower in the hopeless tangle of cars. And the street sign coming up, *Prinsengracht*, and us turning into it. And cold lines of wet houses, and thin ribbons of canals, and pale bridges leaping out of the dark in the lightning.

Three bridges. And we were at the third, the one with the low balustrade, and pulling in. And the same scene again – almost identical; everyone scrambling out and barging against each other while the door was opened. And Ratbag looking slowly about him, at the flying fish on the door, at the little bridge, and then at me, remembering it all, his eyes glittering.

"You knew this last night, didn't you?" he said.

"Not for certain."

"You knew it!" A flash of lightning seemed to yank his eyes right out of his head.

"Ratbag," I said, "I have to – " But I was too busy doing it to supply a running commentary. *Open the map and drop it – twice – if you want a contact.* I wanted one! And the flipping map wouldn't open. It had stuck together like a pizza. I looked frantically up and down the street. A few cars were still cruising past, returning from the concert to this high-class area. And one or two people were splashing past on foot. But the street would soon be still again, still as the grave.

I just hoped some of the night wanderers out there had something to do with us, and managed to pry the map apart and spread it; my hands trembling so much that it fell of its own accord. And I bent and picked it up, and it fell once more – again without help from me.

Then Nellie was with me – the rest having vanished inside – and flapping about like a wet hen. "Nicky, you crazy boy, what are you doing out here?" And she'd peeled the map off the ground and draped it over my arms and bustled me inside.

Into the next great moment of the evening.

Her old man was coming down the stairs, disturbed by the row. And behind him was the guy whose quiet warning had broken up the party last time. The pair of them were staring at Ratbag – staring as if at a ghost – and then they were staring at me.

In a light-headed sort of way I seemed to be staring at myself, at the whole scene, as if in a flashlit photo.

There was the guy Groot had been stalking for a couple of years, without finding. And here was I, huddled like a wet rat in the doorway, with Groot's map draped over my outstretched arms, and Groot's routes carefully inked in, and the big police stamp at the bottom.

Fifteen

"It's OK, Papa, just some friends I brought back – we got caught in the rain," Nellie was saying. And saying it unnecessarily. Max and Saskia were shaking themselves like a couple of wet dogs.

"Well, come in, come in," the old man said. The other guy had been whispering in his ear and the pair of them had come right down the stairs now. "And change out of those clothes – you'll catch cold, all of you."

"A hot shower for me – with your permission?" Max said, mopping his bushy red hair with a handkerchief.

"Of course. Everybody. Nellie, show your friend – Saskia, isn't it? And Max, take the others, you know where, upstairs. Piet will dry your clothes off. You can get into dressing gowns – my goodness," the old man said, "you look as if you've all been in the canal."

He was smiling, very genial, and I remembered him – remembered all of it, the tall narrow house, the beautiful furnishings, the spotlit pictures, even here in the hall. They were all talking English, I suppose for our benefit. And what was coming next – our clothes taken away, us stuck there, unable to leave – would also be for our benefit ...

I was still standing with the map over my arms, and

I began trying to fold it, frantically babbling, "Well, we can't stay. We only came along for the ride. And now we've got to – "

"Nicky, you can't go like that! It's pouring out there. Of course you must get dry," Nellie said. And in half a minute we were all going up the stairs, Saskia, Max, Nellie, Ratbag and myself, with the two others following. I wondered if anybody'd spotted me dropping the book out in the street. And if so, if they'd be doing something about it, and how soon!

The girls were peeling off to one bathroom, and Max and us to another. But it was a tiny one, a shower stall, and Piet – who seemed to be the old man's assistant – said, "No, no, there's another. You can't all get in there." Which was dead true, we couldn't. And Max was already stripping off. So there was nothing for it and we went on, Piet in front now. And I said in Ratbag's ear, "Hang on to your clothes – whatever happens!" And he looked at me and nodded.

"Here," Piet said and opened another door; a bigger room with a bath and a separate shower. "You can use both. And if you'll just give me your wet clothes I'll dry them. Here are bath robes. Maybe they don't fit so well, but it's not a fashion parade."

It was all so sensible and cheerful it was hard to know what to do. Except he hadn't taken Max's clothes, had just left him stripping off. I said, "Well, we'll – we'll just undress by ourselves."

"Ah, you don't like to – OK. Just give me the jackets and I'll wait outside for the rest. You'll put them through the door." He was already helping Ratbag off with his, and there was no way we could get out of it. So he took mine too, and I shut the door and turned the bath on right away, and in the uproar said to Ratbag, "Turn the shower on," and he did.

There was a bolt on the door and I quietly shot it, and said, "Ratbag, we've got to get out of here. Fast. He's waiting out there."

He was looking round the room. There was no window in it, just a little ventilation grill and a cupboard high up near the ceiling. In such an old house it was hard to tell what the room had been before; the ceiling was very lofty. It was filling up with steam now.

Ratbag was staring at the cupboard, and he got on the bath stool and tried to reach it, and couldn't.

"Can you get on my shoulder?" he said.

He stepped down and bent, and I leaned against the wall for support and clambered up on him.

"Jeeze, get your shoes off!" he muttered.

I kicked them off and tried again, and he rose slowly, swearing at my weight, while I teetered up the wall and grasped the knob on the cupboard door. It opened easily. There was a big water tank inside, roaring and gurgling away now at all the stuff coming out of it. I couldn't see anything else in there, all black, but I felt around inside and there was space and a floor to it, so I hoisted myself up and crawled in.

There was no head room and I crouched double and shambled forward on my knees, feeling the dusty floor-boards ahead and reaching out on all sides of me in the dark. Except now I was in it, it wasn't so dark. Light was coming in from somewhere. I felt my way round the tank and saw a faint outline of light, a flat oblong of it in the darkness ahead. And got there, and ran my fingers round it, and identified hinges, and realized it was another cupboard door, the twin of the one behind me in the bathroom.

There was a room below. A room with a light on in it. I tried the door gently, and knew it would open, and wondered if I dare push it a crack to see what was there. And in the same moment realized something else, and scrambled round immediately in the dark and started heading back.

The clot hadn't turned the bath off.

I could hear it still roaring away – maybe even flooding over with him still peering up to see what had happened to me. And roaring far too long for someone just taking a bath. I got to the door and looked down, and there he was staring up at me through clouds of steam. I couldn't even see the bath.

I hissed, "Turn the bath off!" And he did and came back and said, "He's been banging on the door asking for the clothes."

"Tell him we'll bring them when we're through."

He vanished in the steam and I could faintly hear him doing something. Then he came back and peered up. "I don't think he's there," he said.

"OK."

"And the door's locked."

"Yeah, I locked it."

"On the *outside*."

"You sure?"

He went away and came back again. "Yeah," he said.

We peered at each other through the steam.

I said, "Can you get up here?"

He looked about him, and vanished for a moment.

"Catch," he said, and a bath robe came up through the steam. "Hang on your end," he said. I saw him getting up on the bath stool again.

I stretched myself flat and hung out of the cupboard, while he pulled himself up on the bath robe. He used his feet on the wall, slipping a bit on the steamy surface and almost yanking me out. But he reached far enough to get a hand over the edge, and I grabbed him under the shoulder, and he was scrambling in.

"There's a door the other side", I said, "into another room. I don't know what's there."

I shuffled round and led the way and we paused there, listening. The tank was still churning away and we couldn't hear anything above it. I put my ear against the door, careful not to press too hard, and still couldn't hear anything. We crouched there breathing at each other in the dim light of the crack.

"What do you think?" he said.

"If he locked that bathroom door we've had it anyway."

"Yeah."

I listened again at the door, still without hearing anything; so I pushed gently and it popped open. It opened maybe an inch, and I waited. Nothing happened, so I put my eye to the gap and saw a pair of feet.

They were in shiny pointed shoes, and crossed over each other.

I pushed a bit more and saw legs on the end of the

feet, horizontal. And holding my breath, pushed farther. Trousered legs and a stocky body, with a pair of hands interlaced on a stomach. And a bit farther up an East Indian face, fast asleep.

He had his feet on a desk and was stretched back in a chair. I looked as far as I could round the room and saw nobody else, and took my eye from the gap and gave Ratbag a look.

He looked carefully for several seconds, and withdrew.

"I can jump him," he said. "You'll have to hang on my legs while I reach down. If he wakes I'll drop on him."

I looked through the gap again.

The man was directly below; his head *right* below, relaxed backwards and almost touching the wall.

Ratbag was shuffling himself horizontal.

"You sure about this?" I said.

"You got other ideas?"

I hadn't, and he didn't wait. He was flat out now, and he opened the door wide and began feeding himself out. I hung on to his legs and then, as he wriggled more, to his feet. I couldn't see a thing, just felt him straining away. Till he suddenly began kicking and yelled, "Drop me!" and I did, and a fantastic row broke out below.

I stuck my head out the door and saw the back end of him on top of the man. The chair had gone over sideways and the pair of them were half under the desk, the East Indian kicking and wriggling like a cat. Ratbag's long skinny body was shaking and thumping; then the man went still and Ratbag shuffled off him and looked up at me.

"Get down!"

"Is there a key in that door?"

He turned away and said "Yeah" and locked it. "Come on. This geezer won't stay asleep long ... There's a window here," he said.

I could see the window. I could see everything now, upside down, and I didn't like it. He had his arms out, but I couldn't see how he'd catch me. "I'll break my neck!"

"No you won't! Jeeze – I'll make a back, then. You can drop on it."

This didn't seem right, either. His back wasn't particularly soft. But a lot of things weren't right suddenly. I was aware that the tank had stopped gurgling, and I couldn't hear the shower any more. Someone had turned off the shower. Someone was trying to get into the cupboard at the other end ...

Which was about the last coherent thought I had in that position. A number of crazy things happened in rapid succession. The door below began shaking and bulging. Ratbag stopped making a back and ran to it; and then ran back and started shifting the desk there. The East Indian began stirring feebly where the desk had been. Ratbag got the desk in position but almost immediately it was slithering back as the door burst open and four men pushed in.

The East Indian crawled to his knees and swayed a bit, as if praying, his mouth wide open and his eyes raised. His eyes were looking directly into mine, and I looked right back into his. Half of me was hanging in the room and the other half still in the cupboard, where someone was grasping my ankle now.

The situation at both ends was pretty lousy.

Sixteen

There wasn't anything you could call a struggle. They were big heavy men, and two of them jumped Ratbag right away. I saw that but not what happened immediately afterwards because the other two were busy yanking me out of the cupboard. The guy behind me was helping too, and I managed a flying kick backwards just as I came out and gave him a black eye.

I didn't know about the eye till a few minutes later when I saw him glaring at me out of it. We were being held then and the men, more of them now, including Nellie's old man, were ganged up round us. Piet had the map. He'd been tracing the routes marked out on it and was now scrutinizing the police stamp impressed on the bottom.

I could hear music throbbing somewhere and realized the others must have finished their showers and gone to the big living-room I remembered. The old man was aware of it too, and it seemed to bother him. He spoke sharply and a couple of the men left. Then Piet showed him the map and said something in his ear. He examined the map, and then us.

"Who has given you this map?" he said quietly.

"The police," I said right away. "And they're

watching for us outside. And will be here *inside* if we don't come out soon."

He thought about this, his head on one side. Then he gave further rapid orders and more of the men left.

He sucked his knuckles, looking at us.

"I think this is a lie. There have been thefts here, so we have security," he said reasonably. "Whether thieves are making use of you to spy out, or … In any case, *I* will call the police. Meanwhile – " He turned to Piet and broke into fast Dutch, and in a few seconds one of the men had opened the door and was looking out; and in a few seconds more we were being hustled out, too.

The music was louder in the passage, and I opened my mouth to yell, but got a sleeve rammed in it quickly. I bit on the wrist inside the sleeve as hard as I could, and heard the guy softly swearing, but the sleeve stayed in position, and we were still moving, moving upwards now, upstairs. The music was coming from upstairs, and I remembered the flights and half flights we'd gone up before. I could pretty well remember the whole layout of the place now.

We passed the living-room, the music belting out louder now, and I saw a guy stationed there and figured they'd got it locked on the outside till we'd passed. Then more stairs, the stairs to the attic.

It wasn't till we reached that floor that I realized why more trouble hadn't been coming out of Ratbag. They'd hustled me out first, and behind me three of them were frogmarching him. He was silently writhing and kicking, a towel rammed in his mouth. We reached the top floor in a rush, and had to pause there a moment. I remem-

131

bered the attic hadn't occupied the whole floor, and saw now that we weren't going there. There was a door opposite, on the landing. This one was being opened, from the inside, a number of locks being turned.

Then I was in it, and behind me heard struggling and cursing, and managed to twist my head enough to see Ratbag's kicking legs jammed in the doorway, and several of them trying to force him in.

We were in an office, a space-age one, gleaming with keyboards and computer screens. The back wall was a filing system, slotted with computer disks; but as I looked a section of it swung open, and the man who'd let us in hurried through.

Beyond was another room, an incredible room, totally packed. The long side walls were covered with metal shelving, and all the inner space stacked with further columns of shelves, like a library. Except there were no books in the shelves. There were neat plastic packages, piles and piles of them, apparently arranged by size. Two guys were manoeuvring a cart in one of the aisles while another stacked it from the shelves.

I had just a glimpse of this before I heard a hurried *"Nee, nee!"* and a babble of Dutch from the old man, and was swung round to face the other way; in time to see Ratbag on the floor with two of them on top of him, while the door behind him was locked again. Then a blindfold was over my eyes and being tied, tied too tightly, everybody very jittery all of a sudden. And I was being swung round and hustled forward again.

I went through the office, and smelt another odour, evidently the storeroom, and was brushing through an aisle. And through another opening, into a confined space. I was being jostled and bumped there, and realized Ratbag was near and that they were trying to force him in, too.

I was so disorientated, the room seemed to be moving with me. Then there was a sharp muttered conversation and the struggling receded, and there was a purr and the sound of softly-closing doors, and the room did move. It moved downwards. I was in a lift. I said, "Here, what are you – ?" and got the sleeve in my mouth again.

We dropped fast and silently, and I was being pushed out, the sleeve so hard in my mouth it was wide open and I was almost sick. And waiting somewhere while the lift was sent up again. There seemed to be two men with me, and there was a close musty smell in the air. (A basement, with people living close by, though I didn't know it.) In moments the lift was back and the door opening again and slow careful footsteps coming out of it. There was no jostling and struggling this time, and I figured they must be carrying Ratbag. Also that something had happened to him: he was too still.

There was a muttered conversation and the sleeve was taken from my mouth. The guy holding me stepped away, and I said, "Ratbag?"

"He's having a small sleep," Piet's voice said. He must have come down in the lift. I was sure he hadn't been with me before. "He'll wake soon. But listen now. You must be perfectly quiet – quiet as he is, or you'll sleep with him. We are going a short distance, not far, but I must cover your mouth in case you accidentally make a sound. Don't make sounds. Don't make any commotion.

Just walk. If you want you can sleep, and be carried, but it's better if you walk. You want to walk?"

"OK," I said, and licked my lips.

The lift had gone up again, and I knew the two men who'd brought me had gone up with it. I figured only two guys were holding Ratbag, with just Piet to look after me. He didn't want to carry me himself; but he would if he had to.

"A piece of tape," he said, and stuck it on. It was a broad band, from under my nose to my chin. He pressed it tight practically to my ears. "Leave it," he said, as I tried to reach up. "In fact to be on the safe side – " He was tying my hands behind my back, with thin cord – again much too tightly so I knew that despite his reasonable tone he was jittery. I was trussed like a chicken. I felt totally scrambled: blind, dumb, tied.

"Walk now," he said, and tugged my tee-shirt and moved ahead. We moved just a few paces and stopped, and I heard him doing something in front. There was a slight grating and scuffing sound and something moved. "Down steps," he said. "I'll tell you how many," and he counted them off. There were eight. "That's all. Now wait there."

He moved away, and I heard the others shuffling carefully down the steps. Then there was the scuffing sound again, and I knew he was re-closing whatever he'd opened. And he was back, tugging my shirt, and we were moving on. There was a damp heavy smell, a dead smell. We were in a narrow place. The steps we'd come down were of stone, and I could feel stone through my socks now. (And remembered my shoes, left behind in the bathroom!) We seemed to be in a tunnel.

We didn't go far along it; maybe seven or eight yards. I was taking little shuffling footsteps and couldn't tell. Then we'd stopped again, and I heard him rapping on something, a metallic sound. Almost immediately there was an answering rap, fainter, and the same slight grating and scuffing. He'd moved away and I heard a whispered conversation. Then he was back again.

"*Up* steps now," he said softly. "One, two ... " And again there were eight, and we were into a different atmosphere. An airier one. Spicy. A smell of soup somewhere, and something else. Curry? People lived here. The men around me were very quiet now. We were moving in silence. And not moving far.

A lift again, a different kind of lift, slower, very rickety. And we were going up, all of us crammed together so I could feel everybody's breath. Then we were out, and had moved through one door and then another, and the atmosphere changed again, quite suddenly. There was no silence any more, and no tension, so evidently we couldn't be heard here.

A lot of activity was going on, very hurried, of stuff being shifted and dumped. Then we'd left that behind, too, and were in an empty room; one with an echo anyway. And I was being sat on the floor and tied to something, tied very uncomfortably; and sensed from the sounds of straining and bending that the same thing was happening with Ratbag. Then a door closed, and a key turned, and we were alone.

Seventeen

I thought we were alone. I couldn't tell exactly. There was a snuffly kind of breathing, evidently Ratbag's. I listened hard to see if there was anyone else's, and decided there wasn't, so I started wriggling to find out how I was tied. There was a rope across my chest and round both arms. It was secured to something behind. With my elbows I felt a vertical bar there, in the small of my back. It seemed to be iron, and round. The rope moved smoothly on it, so it wasn't going to fray.

I tried to call to Ratbag but only a grunt came out, my mouth stuck tight with the tape. I listened to him a while, wondering if he was taped himself, if the snuffling was him trying to say something. But the breathing was too even for that, so I stretched my legs out to try and touch him. I touched nothing; just bare boards.

I tried to figure the situation out. They'd hustled us out of the house in case the police came looking. It wasn't all they were hustling out. I remembered the frantic activity in the storeroom, and the work evidently going on in the room we'd just come through. They'd switched us from one building – evidently through a tunnel under the basements – to another, a house farther along the row. And they were switching the stuff too. When they were through with that they'd decide what to do about us.

I heard a change in Ratbag's breathing, a choking sound. Then he was threshing about, grunting, and after a moment or two spluttering. "A towel! There was a towel in my mouth!" So he didn't have it taped; and I grunted as hard as I could.

"What the – Hey, OK. You got a blindfold on. Hang on while I try and – "

So *he* wasn't blindfold: eyes free and mouth free. And there must be light in the room for him to see me.

I couldn't tell what he was "trying"; couldn't begin to figure it out. I heard him straining at something, but couldn't identify the pattering sound that came with it. The pattering sounded from the wall behind me. Then it stopped, and he breathed heavily, and began pattering again.

There was presently a slight clang and a sliding sound, and he swore. He breathed deeply again, and got back to the pattering. Then another clang and a soft thud, and he swore some more. He swore for about half a minute.

He paid no attention to my grunts, just got on with what he was doing. He was thrumming something, and presently he said "OK, baby!" and there was a shuffling sound and his hand touching me.

He said, "Hold this between your knees."

I grunted.

"Hold it tight!"

It was something very narrow and sinuous, and I gripped it as hard as I could, and felt it vibrating. He seemed to be grating something, and I knew he'd somehow got a saw there and was cutting through rope. I felt the last strands give, then his hands were fumbling at the back of my head, and the blindfold came off.

The first thing I saw was his face covered with blood. It was streaming down from his forehead. His mouth was hanging loosely to one side. "It's OK," he said crookedly through it. "Damn thing hit me on the head. I hooked it off the wall with my feet and couldn't get out the way. It's only a nick."

It was worse than a nick. It was a deep gash, but he didn't seem to know it yet. What had hit him was a bow saw, a huge old one with jagged teeth. As he stripped the tape off my mouth I looked up and saw where it had come from. There was a collection of old tools up on the wall, mounted between pairs of hooks.

They were so high he must have practically stood on his head, all his weight on his bound wrists as his feet pattered backwards up the wall to reach it. They hadn't tied him round the chest – maybe because he was unconscious and they were in a hurry. His hands had been bound behind him and they'd run a rope through and tied him to a support. He'd cut the support rope, but had needed my knees to get at the one between his wrists.

I looked round the room while he untied me. The only light filtered through a dirty glass slit over the door. It was so dim it threw most of the room into shadow. We'd been tied to a couple of iron frames sticking out of the wall. They were about six feet apart and supported a bulky contraption between them. Apart from that, and the collection of tools on the wall, the room was empty. Bare boards, no furniture, no windows.

My head was singing a bit, but I had a dreamlike feeling I'd been here before; was certain of it. And in the same moment remembered – the attic room, the museum room, in the other house. I muttered crazily to myself.

"What other house?" Ratbag said.

He had no idea he wasn't still in it. The last thing he remembered was kicking someone half-way across a room, then getting cracked on the jaw and having a needle shoved in his arm. They'd drugged him. I brought him up to date as I went prowling round the room.

There *had* been a window – in the other room, at least. I'd leaned out of it. Then I remembered it wasn't a window but a door, a double one, of wood, and someone – Max, Danny, Nellie? – had hunted and fiddled about to open it. I was terribly mixed up, couldn't remember the order of events; racked my brains to try and recall them now. The window, the opening anyway, had been at the far end of the room away from the door.

I went to the far end and felt there. And found it. The wooden projection stood out from the wall, so heavily shadowed you couldn't see it. I ran my hand round the edge, then bent and felt underneath, and found a metal knob. The end of a bolt. Of course, there'd been bolts! They'd drawn bolts. I levered and pulled, and it came easily, and the door moved. It moved enough to show it was half of a pair of doors, a crack suddenly appearing between the two.

I moved to the other side, found the bolt there and shifted that one too. Both halves bulged outwards. I shoved them but got nowhere, the doors still stuck at the top, and I realized there must be another pair of bolts up there. And remembered, yes, that night, everyone laughing and larking about with a ladder.

I went hunting frantically in all the dark places for a ladder, and couldn't find one. No ladder here.

Ratbag was staring stupidly at me, dabbing his head. He seemed to be swaying on his feet. He didn't look too good. I said, "Ratbag, can you get me on your shoulders again – the way we did it in the bathroom?"

He didn't say anything, just looked at me dully, and bent over by the double doors, and I went up on him.

He raised me slowly, wobbling, and I groped at the top of the door and found the bolt and slid it, and we did the other, and both doors moved – moved ponderously, vibrating slightly, but without trouble and without creaking, just a soft rumble. I came down fast, and we pushed them wider. The massive doors stretched from just below the ceiling to about a foot off the floor. The whole wall opened, and it was all sky there. A huge mass of night sky, with the glow of a city, and a damp breeze blowing.

Ratbag swayed in the opening, and I hung on to him, afraid he'd fall out, and got him to kneel on the floor. There was a little sill there, and I knelt by it myself and looked down. A narrow slit of canal winked far below – five floors at least. The dark shape of a barge was moored there.

And I remembered it, remembered as if in a dream. All exactly as before! And across the narrow slit the same row of tall shuttered buildings as before. Except they weren't the same, couldn't be ... I stared, and shook my head, and stared again. Nellie and Max were standing

140

opposite. They were standing not ten yards away. They were in a lighted window and behind them people were dancing. They were one floor below, but at the other side of the canal. Everything in reverse …

I felt totally disorientated, couldn't grasp it; but at the same time remembered – one lift going down and another coming up, with a tunnel in between. We'd gone *under* the canal, were on the other side of it.

Ratbag heard me muttering, watching my lips like a puzzled dog as he crouched beside me. He wasn't taking it in; his eyes hazy with pain, his crooked jaw trembling slightly. All of him seemed to be trembling. Whatever drug they'd given him was wearing off, and he was in worse condition now than when he'd come to. He'd had the energy to act then. He seemed dopey with pain now, his brain sluggish.

Mine wasn't. I seemed to be seeing everything clearly for the first time. OK, we were at the other side of the canal. And they'd left us temporarily to attend to more urgent business. And they wouldn't leave us for long. That was for certain. We had to be out fast.

Also, I could see how now. If only the thing worked. If I could figure out the way to work it …

I could see the pole sticking obliquely up over the attic opposite, and leaned out to peer above our own opening. The same kind of pole, the iron hook at the end blackly outlined against the sky. I couldn't see any rope attached to it but knew it must be there. I pulled Ratbag away from the opening, set him to listen at the door, and went hunting round the room for rope.

I couldn't see the angle between wall and ceiling

where the rope had to be, but felt the wall and found where it descended; also realized the function of the bulky contraption between the bars we'd been tied to.

The thing was covered with tarpaulin tightly lashed round with cord. I couldn't find the end of the cord, got the saw to it, and in seconds was peeling the tarpaulin off. There was a drum of heavy rope underneath, a winch full of it – the same kind of winch as in the other attic. There must be a wheel on the ceiling, but I couldn't see it. The rope would run up through the wheel and cross to the double doors to exit along the pole to the hook on the end. I couldn't see any of it, couldn't even find the handle to unwind the thing.

I felt around and found something else. Iron cog wheels at one end of the drum. A whole series of them, interlocked. I brushed my fingers over them, found an iron rod running down from the biggest and followed it with my hand. It made a right-angle turn underneath. There was a wooden roller on the end, a kind of sleeve, that revolved freely. I yanked down to pull it loose but it wouldn't come; then realized it must be hinged sideways, and tugged that way and it swung out easily. The handle.

I levered it this way and that, felt the cog wheels ease a bit, but couldn't move them. The thing was locked. Yes, as in the other attic; and they hadn't managed to unlock it. I frantically tried to figure it out, felt round every part of the winch. No obvious lock. No chain of any kind. Each cog wheel meshed closely with the others, and a handle to turn the main one and set the whole thing going.

It had jammed somewhere; was a museum piece after all; wasn't intended for use any more; was probably blocked solid with rust. I told myself not to panic, stepped back and rubbed the dirt off my hands, and tried to think it through. Suddenly realized it wasn't dirt on my hands but grease, and peered at them, held them right up to my eyes, even smelt the fingers. Clean grease, new grease, no sign or smell of rust at all. Whatever was checking the winch, it wasn't rust. The thing was kept in good order. A bit of grit must be jamming one of the cogs.

I began feeling the separate teeth, then realized it would take too long and tried another way, rocking the handle with one hand and holding the cog train with the other to feel which part was jamming. Right away I found it. A big thing like a prong was stuck at an angle between the teeth of the main cog.

I touched it, felt it, couldn't see it. Couldn't see a damn thing! But I followed it up with my hand, felt a hinge and a change of direction, then another hinge and a solid horizontal bar. I could see that. It looked like one of the tools, except it wasn't on hooks but fixed directly to the wall. I pulled it, and everything moved. The hinges moved, the prong lifted upwards, and the winch was free. It was a brake. The thing had had its brake on!

I turned the handle and the whole mechanism softly rumbled, turning easily. There was a slapping sound on the ceiling and something moved there. I carried on turning, and in a moment or two was aware that something was moving outside, too. The hook was lowering.

I could hardly believe it. I said, "Ratbag!" and he came over at once and stood watching me, dully. I'd wanted him to grab the hook but I saw he wasn't up to it, and said instead, "Hang on to the handle. Just don't let it go!" and went and tried myself.

The hook was too far out, and I scrambled back in the room and picked the bits of cord off the floor and quickly tied them together. It took a couple of goes, using the cord as a lasso, but I made it and pulled the hook towards me.

It was a big thing, almost the size of a car wheel, and suspended not on one rope, as I'd thought, but on two. There was an iron ring at the top of the hook, and a grooved wheel was mounted sideways in it. The ropes went round the wheel. I couldn't pull the hook quite in, and told Ratbag to unwind more rope. It still wouldn't come.

"Keep going," I said.

He unwound so much rope it began looping down from the ceiling. The hook still wouldn't budge. Blocked somewhere. I hung out the window again and looked up at the ropes. They were coming from two separate wheels set closely together in a little gap above the opening. I hugged the hook with one hand and felt the ropes with the other. Both were taut, and I pulled one. The hook rose, almost yanking me out. I switched fast to the other rope. The hook lowered with a jerk.

I thought about this. There had to be a block and tackle on the ceiling. There had to be. The rope left the drum in a single length but evidently went through some kind of mechanism that doubled it. Two ropes came out the top of the window anyway. Pull one of them and the hook was raised, pull the other and it lowered …

I let the hook go but hung on to the lasso and laid it

on the floor. Then I went over to the door and put my ear to it. We couldn't have been in the room long but all sense of time had left me. I didn't know how much row I'd be making; didn't want anyone listening the other side of the door.

I couldn't hear anyone there. Muffled vibrations came through it – of hurried footsteps, wheels rumbling, stuff being shifted about; all distant.

Ratbag was watching me like a zombie, still hanging on to the handle. I took it off him and began winding rope in. The loop snaked up off the floor and I kept winding till I saw the hook jerk and the lasso twitch. Then I stopped and began unwinding. I unwound about six feet, and put the brake on.

In the same moment the moon came out, and a filmy luminescence swam over the room. It was so weird we stood stock still, staring at each other. His eyes were dull, his jaw still wobbling.

"What you trying to do?" he said.

"We got to go out there, Ratbag. We got to go down on the hook together."

"Doesn't someone have to work the handle?" His mouth seemed full of stones.

"I don't think so. I don't know. I'm going out to see."

I put him on the handle anyway, in case I was wrong, and went over to the window and pulled the hook in. It still wouldn't come all the way, so I tugged at the down rope, and it came. I got it over the sill and into the room and lowered it gently to the floor. The underside edge was flat so it stood upright without wobbling, and I stood in it, and pulled the up rope and it moved.

It moved at once, lifting me off the floor and sliding over to the sill where it dragged, so that I tilted sharply and hung on tight, too tight, to the up rope, and found myself jerked upwards a couple of feet, and swinging clean over the sill out into the moonlight.

I hung on both ropes, not pulling, just balancing, my head swimming, and I thought, Oh God, I've done it now.

Eighteen

The hook was twirling, and I shut my eyes. My stomach had given a single massive heave and I felt the whole world spinning; like a double somersault under water when you can't figure out which way up you are.

I swung for about half a minute, then felt maybe I wasn't swinging so much and opened my eyes, and found I wasn't swinging at all. I was standing in the air, sixty or seventy feet above the canal and six feet out from the building. Nothing was moving; everything gravely still, except a few wisps of cloud scudding under the moon.

My hands were over my head clutching the ropes, and I had the craziest series of thoughts. I thought, well the rain's stopped. I thought, Nellie and Max will see me standing here. Then I saw they weren't there any more. They were dancing with the others. A few more people had arrived and I could see them clearly – as clearly as I saw Ratbag, standing by the handle and staring out at me. I thought, the party hasn't broken up then. The police haven't gone in. So they can't have followed us. And it hasn't happened. None of it has happened. It's a dream. I'm dreaming it.

But I knew I wasn't – everything too soberly detailed.

Fresh details were still hitting me. The rain hadn't quite stopped, for instance. A few drops were still in the air and I was shivering in the cool breeze. And my stockinged feet were hurting in the hard iron curve of the hook. And the canal wasn't right below me. The stern end of the barge was there. No, it was all happening, so I got on with what I had to do.

I'd paid out six feet of rope off the drum, so I went down what I thought was that distance, a few inches at a time; and the rope checked then, without shuddering or skidding, but without going any farther either. The block and tackle held, and the brake held, very firmly. I went up again, just as easily, the mechanism so finely balanced it was no effort at all; and drew level with the sill and saw Ratbag still staring out at me from the handle.

I scooped up the lasso and tossed the cord in the room, and told Ratbag to pull in; and in seconds was standing there with him.

"Was there any movement on the handle?"

"None."

"We can do it then."

"Together?"

"Yeah. Can you carry me on your back?"

He just goggled at me, swaying.

He was going to have to carry me so I didn't bother explaining. I couldn't carry *him*. My feet had hurt too much just carrying myself. He couldn't handle the ropes, anyway. I went over to the winch and let the brake off and began winding out rope. It came snaking off the ceiling and bundled in coils on the floor. I unwound almost the lot, leaving maybe ten feet, and put the brake on and went over to the hook again.

"I don't have to get on your shoulders. I'll hang on your back," I told him. He was looking terrible. The blood had dried on his face but it was still a gooey mess on his forehead. His eyes were staring and his mouth wouldn't close. "Bend a bit," I told him. And he did, and I got on, wrapping my legs round him. He staggered, but supported me. "Now stand in the hook."

He got one foot in but couldn't manage the other and reached up for the ropes.

"*Leave* the ropes. Don't even touch them! Hang on to the ring. Bend and hang on to it tight, both hands."

He did, got both feet in somehow and crouched there, with the hook wobbling but staying upright.

"OK?" I said in his ear.

He mumbled something I couldn't catch, but he was hanging on, and with both hands. "It bangs a bit on the sill," I said, "so *really* tight."

Then I wrapped my legs more securely round him and reached up for the ropes and balanced on them.

"Shut your eyes," I said, and pulled, and we went. We went sliding over the floor, tilted at the sill, and were over it and swinging out in the night.

I kept my eyes closed while we swung and twirled. We were still twirling when I opened them. I didn't look round me or below. I kept my eyes on the ropes, and my hands hanging there, and waited till they stabilized, and started down.

We dropped smoothly, a few inches at a time, and passed the shutters of the next floor down, and then the one after. Big iron rings were stapled into the wall by each pair of shutters. They stuck out a bit but didn't interfere with the hook. We passed the next pair, and I stopped and looked below. Two floors to go. Twenty or thirty feet. The barge was right underneath.

I'd seen from above that it was in darkness, and covered with a tarpaulin-lashed load. Now I was nearer I saw the load didn't completely cover it. Also it wasn't in total darkness. A little structure I hadn't spotted before was perched on the stern, and a dim glimmer of light was coming from it.

I peered hard. The light was coming from a window. I could see the faint square reflection of it on the brick wall of the building. And the window was open: a curl of smoke wafted up from it. I sniffed. A cigar. The same kind of acrid smell that was in all the cafés. A little tinny sound wafted up with it, that I couldn't at first make out; then identified as a radio. Someone was down there on the barge, smoking a cigar and listening to the radio.

This was no good; no good at all. The barge was lashed tight to the building. I could see one of its mooring ropes now, slanted upwards to a ring in the wall. There was no water in between. We'd either have to drop on the barge or somehow get past it; which would mean passing the window. It was right under the hook.

I tried to figure this out, and felt Ratbag wriggling and hissing underneath me.

"Hang on. Just a bit longer," I said in his ear.

He nodded, still trying to ease his back. I took the weight off a bit, balancing on both ropes and lifting myself slightly. But this was too risky, so I tried reaching one of the rings beside the shutter, and made it, and hung on that a moment.

I wondered, then, if I couldn't use it some other way: push myself away from it along the wall to the next ring. I peered sideways. A double line of rings ran down each building in the terrace. It was some way to the next one. I tried reaching out, one hand on the ring and the other clawing along the wall and saw I wasn't going to make it, and experimentally pushed off to see if I could swing myself that far. The hook swung, and I gripped Ratbag tightly, reaching out, and still couldn't make it.

The hook went on swinging, and Ratbag went on hissing; more urgently now.

I saw how we *might* do it, though. With enough momentum a good swing could carry us right past the barge. We'd have to do it well above the window so the old man couldn't see us. Which meant doing it from the ring of the first story, and dropping off from that height. Twelve or fifteen feet. Not such a long drop. Not such a huge splash. Not if he kept listening to his radio.

I told Ratbag what I planned, said we'd have to try a dummy run first to see how far we could swing, and to hang on.

He just hissed some more, and I pushed off. The hook swung again, and I gave a push the other way as we came back, and felt the ropes creak and shudder above. It took three swings to get clear of the barge, and even then we didn't clear it by much – maybe a yard. It looked like the best we were going to do, but we'd still be swinging out as we dropped off, which should increase the distance.

I saw we couldn't drop off together. I'd go first, and he'd have to wait for the next swing before following. I told him this, and grabbed at the ring to slow us; and when we'd stabilized again, began lowering away.

We went down another story, and stopped, and were so near the window I could see right in. There was a potted geranium on a window ledge, and beyond it part of an old guy in a rocking chair. All I could see of him was the top of a bald head, but I bent and saw he had a newspaper stretched out in front of him: he was reading it through a pair of glasses perched on his nose. A bit of cigar was clamped tight in his mouth. I couldn't see the radio but I could certainly hear it better. The tinny transistor sound was turned up so high it was distorting. He must be half deaf. Good.

"OK, Ratbag," I said, "let's go"; and started the swing. We swung twice, and I gave the final push and got my hands down lightly on his shoulders, unwrapped my legs, and at the end of the third swing dropped.

I dropped cleanly, my legs straight down to make less of a splash, but made one all the same, and plunged in, deep, deep. The water was black, icy cold, and I began swimming right away, under it, so he wouldn't drop on me. I counted twenty and came up and shook the water out of my eyes and saw the idiot still swinging. He'd missed one chance and was looking round behind him trying to judge the next. I saw he wasn't going to make it. The thing was slowing down, needed another shove for more momentum.

I hissed up at him, "Push off again!"

And he did. Pushed off. From the hook. He didn't so much fall as tumble. He seemed to snag on the mooring rope and bounce off it to thump the rounded stern of the barge. He caught it such a clout the thing actually swayed. Then he slithered off it and went under. I trod water for a few seconds, waiting for him to come up, and when he didn't started swimming over there. He surfaced a few strokes ahead of me, not moving much, just getting his head above water.

I said, "You OK, Ratbag?"

He didn't answer, didn't even turn towards me, just stayed in the same place as if looking for something below.

I swam up to him and got an arm under his shoulders. "Are you hurt?"

"I don't know, I hit my back, I don't know." He seemed dazed and the words came in such a slow sort of jumble I could hardly catch them.

"Lean back and I'll tow you. We've got to get the hell out of here."

We had. An oblong section of brick wall had lit up as the cabin door opened. The old man came out. The barge was still rocking and the thump must have disturbed him. I got an arm under Ratbag's chin and started towing him away. I couldn't see the old guy properly. He seemed to be hanging on to his head, and at the same time fumbling with something. It wasn't till a torch beam came on and I saw lines streaking through it that I realized it was raining again. Raining hard. He had a newspaper on his head.

He swung the torch about, examining the stern, and then looked up. The hook was still swinging, and his torch found it and carried on up the ropes to the misty outline of the open shutters high above. He let out a yell then. But he still couldn't make out what had happened. Between hanging on to the newspaper, flashing his torch round the boat and staring upwards, it took him some time to figure it out. Then he began peering over the side and flashing the torch there. But we were out of range then, and in half a minute all I knew about him was a tiny blur of moving light and a voice shouting in the dark.

The rain was hissing down on the water and I hauled Ratbag backwards through it. He was in a bad way at the time, but I didn't know how bad. I had no clear idea of anything then, even where I was going, except it had to be away from here.

Nineteen

I knew there had to be an opening off the cutting into the main canals – to the Prinsengracht on the right and some other one to the left. I was keeping to the left, and presently saw it, a gap between buildings, and turned in there.

The dome of a bridge loomed a few yards ahead and I swam under it and took a breather there. It was just a long brick archway, nothing to hang on to, so I trod water and supported Ratbag in the dark.

"How's your back?"

"My legs, not working," he mumbled.

"How are your arms?"

"I don't know, I think the left, I don't know." He was slurring the words so much they barely made sense.

I swore a bit. "OK, stay still. We'll rest."

I tried to figure out where we were. I could see another opening at the other side of the cutting, with another bridge there. It must be the one carrying the road alongside the Prinsengracht, the one we'd driven down; the one we'd walked down last night.

The other way, under our own bridge, I saw rain spattering a wider stretch of water, the next main canal. We had to turn in there, and get out where we could.

Now I'd stopped swimming the water was very cold, and I was shivering in it; and felt Ratbag, in my arms, racked by even harder trembling. I couldn't keep him in much longer. I wondered how I was going to get him out.

I was wondering that when the motor launch started up.

It started up the other side of the cutting, in the Prinsengracht, and took off immediately.

I was so scrambled I took off myself, hauling Ratbag on his back and kicking off right away. But almost at once I realized there was no time, that we'd barely clear the bridge, would be seen threshing in the water if it came this way. I pulled in to the side again and held him tight against the brick curve, his head just above water.

Only moments later the boat turned in from the Prinsengracht.

The first I saw of it was a big white prow, and windscreen wipers going fast in front of a dimly-lit cabin. Then its searchlight came on. The light was mounted on a framework over the cabin and cut blindingly through the rain. The boat just nosed into the cutting and swung there a moment before turning to point in the direction of the barge. It moved along there, but didn't move far, and I heard its engine throbbing; then it reversed and began turning slowly towards us.

"Hold your breath, Ratbag. We're going under," I said, and pulled him down with me.

The boat burbled slowly under the bridge. I could hear its screw churning under water; churning powerfully but very slowly. It seemed hardly to be moving. I counted to fifty, then sixty, and could have held it longer but felt Ratbag heaving in my arms, and came up slowly with him.

The thing seemed to be everywhere, filling the archway, throbbing and burbling with a colossal stink of diesel. It was inching along, about half-way through, the searchlight pointing out the other end so they couldn't see us. The sheer white side crawled past, and I felt the turbulence of the water somewhere under my stomach as the screw drew level.

The launch stopped again soon after. I saw it nosing this way and that, the searchlight pointing left and right along the canal. Then it made a circle, the light sweeping round to enter the tunnel again, so we took a lungful of diesel and went under.

The engine note altered as it came towards us, and then it was rumbling powerfully past, the screw threshing faster. I felt Ratbag begin to heave and choke again, but held him down all the same; held him down till I was sure the screw was past, and we bobbed up like corks, Ratbag spluttering and retching.

He was sick there in the water. I couldn't help him. The archway was still reeking with diesel smoke but it was all we had to breathe.

From the boat's wake I knew it had turned towards the barge again, and from the throaty roar of the engine that it had speeded up. "OK," I said. It would stop at the barge, take a little time there. It couldn't turn in the cutting; would have to back again if it wanted to come this way. Now was the time to move.

He was still throwing up, but I had no choice and put

him on his back again. I even got him to move his left arm, to warm him up and give him something to do, while I used my own right and kicked off as hard as I could. The brick wall of the tunnel went slowly past, and we came out of it into the main canal.

It seemed so wide there, after the slit I'd come out of, I didn't know which way to turn. The glow of the city was in the sky everywhere, radiant after the darkness of the bridge and the gloom of the cutting. There seemed to be more floodlit domes and steeples to the right so I began heading there.

The emerald-lit trees were lined either side of the canal but it was no fairyland now. The rain was still lashing down and there wasn't a dog in sight – not even a car. The canal was dotted with a few moored boats, all in darkness, and with some crazy idea that I had to stay away from boats I swam to the middle of the canal. Then realized we were more exposed there if anyone came round looking in a car, and kicked towards the side again.

Ratbag had stopped doing anything now, except retching a bit and shuddering. I slowly kicked past a few boats, and realized I was getting exhausted myself and needed a rest; and pulled in to the lee of the next boat and bobbed there while I looked round for something to hang on to.

The boat was hitched to a bollard, so I pulled close to the side and reached up and hung on to its rope. Just with the effort of doing it I knew I couldn't go on much longer. My arms and legs were trembling, and not from cold now but sheer fatigue. I'd been going as hard as I could and was dead beat.

I'd had some idea, in making for the lights, of getting right into town, but I knew I couldn't do it. I could barely hang on to the rope. We had to get out. And I couldn't see how to do that, either. The canal side was vertical, and steep. I couldn't leave him in the water while I tried to get out myself.

I heard a car ahead, and slipped off the rope till it whooshed past, then reached up again; just in time for another, that I hadn't heard, coming from behind. It splashed slowly past, and the driver didn't see me. I saw him, hunched forward and peering through his wipers in the rain. And I saw something else. The little old Renault was lurching on the cobbles, its headlights bucking up and down. They flashed, just for an instant, on a flight of steps. The steps ran down from the canal side. Fifty yards or so ahead.

Ratbag had been very quiet for a bit, and I looked at him. His eyes were closed, mouth open, rain bouncing off his face. In the greenish light he looked like a corpse.

I said, "Ratbag."

His eyes fluttered but didn't open.

"Don't go to sleep, Ratbag."

I had an idea you had to keep them awake, in shock: he seemed to be in heavy shock.

"Open your eyes. Look at me."

He managed to flicker his eyes a bit and close them again.

"Ratbag, listen. There's steps ahead. We're getting out there. You've got to move your arm. Let me see you move it."

Some kind of sound came out of him but no movement. I thought, oh jeeze, and got him moving myself. I pushed out from the boat and lugged him backwards. He was a dead weight in the water and his head went under a couple of times. My legs were so tired they didn't want to move any more. I forced them to move, kicking past the boat, and a little gap of oily water, and two or three more boats, desperately wanting to rest again, just for a minute, knowing I couldn't, that I mustn't, that he was in bad shape here. And came to the steps, and saw they ended in a landing stage, just above the water. And got my hand on it and rested there, almost sick with relief.

"We made it, Ratbag. We're at the steps."

His lips moved, but no sound came out.

"I'll get you out in a minute. I'll do it."

I raised his good hand to the stage so he could feel it, and tried to get him to hang on there, but he couldn't. So I rested a while longer, and clutched his tee-shirt with one hand and hauled myself up with the other, and hung there a moment, twisting round to lie flat so I could hold him up in the water.

I just lay there on the stage, absolutely done in and with my breath sobbing. His head was flopping loosely in the water and his shirt had come riding up round his neck where I held it. I didn't know how to pull him out, frontwards or backwards. I thought maybe the front would do least damage, and presently began trying that way. I got my arms under his shoulders and managed to haul the top of him on the stage; then hitched at his jeans and slithered the rest of him on, and crouched panting over him as he lay in a wet huddle, face downwards.

I looked at the steps and thought I'd better go up myself first. My legs were so rubbery they wouldn't hold me, so I went up on hands and feet, and rested at the top.

The street was lined with cars, so I had protection if one came round looking, and I raised myself and saw the hut. I ducked down as a car approached, and let it go past, and wiped the rain out of my eyes and looked again. The hut was in a patch of shade between trees. It had a lifebelt hanging on it. I went slowly towards it and saw it was a three-sided shelter, open to the canal. There was a bench inside and another lifebelt hanging on the wall.

I took in all this, in a dopey kind of way, and went back and down the steps again. He was lying in the same heap but I saw his shoulders rising and falling so he was breathing. It was all he was doing, and I crouched down beside him and said, "Ratbag."

Rain was streaming off his face, his eyes shut and his mouth open.

I said, "Ratbag, I've got to get you up the steps. There's a shelter there. Can you hear me?"

A murmur came out of him, and I put my face next to his.

"If I put your arms over my shoulders, could you keep them there?"

"Yeah yeah," he said. I thought he said.

I levered him up, frontwards, and got his arms there, and his head fell over my shoulder.

"Try a bit, Ratbag. Try and hang on."

"Yeah," he said huskily in my ear.

I don't know if he tried, but nothing happened, and

somehow I got him up myself, having to hold him round the back; not wanting to hold too hard but having to, he kept slipping. And started backwards up the steps, dragging him.

I had to sit down half-way, his head flopping over my shoulder like a giant baby's, and when I started up again suddenly caught sight of his feet dragging bumpety-bump up the steps, and his crazy old sneakers, one blue and the other red, and for some reason began crying. I don't know why I did, and it didn't stop me, and I got to the top and waited there, looking round and hitching him up a bit more. Then I got him to the shelter and laid him on the floor.

I'd more or less stopped thinking. I sat on the bench a bit, trying to pull myself together, but all I thought was, well I got him out the rain. It wasn't really thinking. A mad sort of fantasy was going wearily on in my mind, that I seemed to have heard about or read about, but could barely understand. It all kept going on there, in no particular order.

A cheering concert with a Queen, and someone swinging on a hook, and an audition with a famous musician, and swimming in a canal, and being locked up in a room. Then it slowly sank in on me that it had really happened, and to me; that I was sitting on a public embankment in a town of a million people with taxis and hotels and a police force, and there had to be something I could do about it.

I think I had that in mind.

I don't know what I had in mind.

I was out of the shelter and stumbling along the

canalside, going towards the lights of town.

I'd been dodging every car so far but I didn't dodge this one. It came splashing along fast and I jumped into the road, waving, and it narrowly missed me, slewing round and skidding to a halt on the cobbles.

The driver had wound down his window and was cursing and yelling at me in Dutch.

I said, "English, do you speak English?"

He said, "Ja," and then, "What is your trouble?"

I think, in all that amazing jumble, I must already have recognized what the car was. It was a white one, a Volkswagen, and on the side it said *POLITIE*. Police.

I was sitting in a blanket with a mug of coffee when they wheeled him through on an iron bed. He was already in an operating gown. They'd cleaned him up and brought him to, so he was quite conscious but very drowsy. They'd given him his pre-operation injection and he'd be under the anaesthetic in a few minutes. He was grinning in a lopsided way and not looking quite at me but at the wall behind. "No numbers," he said crazily.

"Yeah, OK. Don't talk, Ratbag."

But he did and I put my head down and tried to make it out.

"I didn't want it anyway," he said.

"Don't worry about it. They'll fix you up."

"He can make some other genius happy today."

It wasn't till he was out of the room I realized he'd been talking about van Bergh and tomorrow's audition. It had still been on his mind. And he was still mixed up. So much had happened today he thought it was already tomorrow.

Then I looked where he'd been looking at the wall behind me and saw an electronic clock there without numbers. The two hands were together, just a bit off vertical: five past one. Five past one in the morning. And I realized I was the mixed-up one, not him. There'd never been anything wrong with his numbers. Tomorrow was already here.

Twenty

They drove me back about three o'clock in the morning, and I had the big room at the Grand Hotel Tivoli to myself. It seemed strange. It seemed unreal. I didn't seem to want to turn the light off. I didn't even want to go to bed.

They'd got a copper outside the door so I wasn't frightened. I just didn't know what to do with myself. I felt dazed and empty. I walked round the room a bit, and sat on my bed, and then on his. I looked at his trumpet.

I don't remember getting into bed but Groot woke me there at twelve, from a heavy sleep, and I saw my clothes slung on the other bed and him sitting among them. He'd taken the breakfast tray off the waiter and brought it in himself.

"You have slept well," he told me.

He didn't look as if he had himself.

"How is he?" I said.

"Resting. It was a long operation, his spine, several ribs ... They say he did well, a strong boy."

"How's his jaw?"

"Strapped up for now. Everything can't be done at once."

"But will he be able to – "

"For sure, for sure. I'm one hundred per cent certain."

I remembered he'd been that certain before, one hundred per cent, so maybe you needed two hundred out of him. But I ate my breakfast all the same, ravenously hungry, while he filled me in – on things I knew as well as those I didn't, so he was evidently feeling his sleeplessness.

He'd forgotten I'd been with them when they raided the tunnel. The alarm of the three families in the other house, who'd not known what had been going on above and below them. Even the East Indian's own family, in the caretaker's flat, hadn't known. The smell of curry still there ... And the millions of dollars' worth of heroin, and the computer accounts of the hundreds of small dealers ...

I hadn't heard about the old man, caught at the private airfield, with his private jet actually revving up for take-off. And I didn't even care. I didn't care anything about the whole heroin business, though I know I should have done. Ratbag had been the one to care about that, and look where it had got him.

He was three weeks in Amsterdam and then another four in hospital in England before they let him out. Even then it was weeks more before he was out of the wheelchair. He was practicing his trumpet, though, long before that. I'd brought it with me when I left Amsterdam the following day, and given it to his old lady. She seemed scared of it, didn't even want to touch the old battered case, and I remembered who it had belonged to before Ratbag had it; so I handed it over to Skinhead, who kept it locked up.

I wasn't supposed to talk about the details till after the trial (the travel agent in England was also in custody), but how do you keep quiet with someone like Sammy around? He kept on and on about everything. *How* had the police lost us that night? If Groot thought the house was one of those in the Prinsengracht why hadn't he got them all covered when we disappeared? Why hadn't he got the whole police force out looking for us?

(Well, he practically had: the *Politie* cars and extra crews were racing round everywhere, including the one I'd nearly given a heart attack to when I suddenly jumped out in the road.)

Even crazy little things like our jackets and my shoes, and how I'd got them back ...

He doesn't stop, he just keeps on. It's the way he is.

These days he keeps on about birds, and all the new ones he's spotted with his binoculars; and I let him rattle on. I advise him to stick to birds and stay away from buses.

And Skinhead: only smiles out of him these days. He knows the music fund will never need topping up again; not after the check from Holland. And his brass section is still the best around. Even though he's lost his star performer ...

Yes, he's lost him. I think we all have, really. He's flown high, has Ratbag. I mean, Peewee. And it happened very fast, like everything else with him. He was still in his wheelchair when the agents came running; and not long out of it when he got his first contract.

That was the result of the van Bergh interview (that the fans know all about) when the old man named him the most "dynamic" performer he'd ever heard.

And Ratbag was right, he *would* have got the scholarship; the old man said so. But also right (as van Bergh said too) to go his own way. He'd always done that anyway. Just as he'd always known, even in those lost crazy days at school, that he had to "do something".

Of course everyone claims now how well they knew him; and I don't know whether to laugh or be sick when I hear it. *I* never knew him, and I don't know if I do now. So there's not much I can add that's not already known.

Except maybe one thing. I know he tried to find his old man, to have him cured (this was right after he made the charts, when he was suddenly in the money). He had private detectives looking, and they found him just before he died, in a hospital somewhere; he'd been out of his mind for weeks so he never knew that "Paulie" had really got to the end of the rainbow and had really found the pot of gold.

I don't know what Ratbag felt about this, or even if he told his old lady. It's hard to know with him, he's still so secretive. I see him, of course, when he's around, but I feel – strange with him. It's not that he's changed towards me. It's just that now he's so famous I feel ... I don't know what I feel.

I get all his records: they're sent to me. But one time

168

he wanted me to have something special, and sent a car for me.

I'd been there before – several times – but a place like that still knocks you over: the huge drive, the park, the pool, the whole fantastic property. He was recording in the studio when I got there, but he told the crew to hold it and put the new one on for me, the video version. It wasn't coming out till the following month, I remember, so apart from people in the business I was the first to hear it. *Screamin' High* ...

It's sold over twenty million now, but that's not the reason I remember it; though I knew right away it would be his biggest seller. It wasn't that. It was the strange way he looked at me while the introduction was playing, that weird wailing and screaming and laughing ...

I felt strange myself when I got home. I felt restless, unreal – the way I'd felt in the room in Amsterdam that night.

I couldn't stay home, and went out and started walking, and found myself walking past a familiar house: big, gaunt, Victorian, four stories, five if you counted the cellar.

I paused outside it, then walked slowly up the path and pushed the side door open. There was no one there and I walked round and found the coal cellar. It was locked, and I put my eye to a crack and tried to see in, but I couldn't, all dark there. I could remember it, though. The two iron beds, the table, the sooty flag-stones, the naked bulb. I remembered saying to him, "Can't you get something better?" And he'd said, "Yeah, I'll get a palace! I'll give it to her."

And he had. He'd done it.

I looked at the back garden. The same straggly looking mess, with the flaky rose trellis, and the hut beyond ...

I could hardly believe it. I hardly can now.